Before
MIDNIGHT

Before MIDNIGHT

CAMERON DOKEY

Simon Pulse

NEW YORK LONDON TORONTO SYDNEY NEW DELHI

SIMON PULSE

An imprint of Simon & Schuster Children's Publishing Division

1230 Avenue of the Americas, New York, NY 10020

This Simon Pulse paperback edition March 2021

Text copyright © 2010 by Cameron Dokey

Cover photograph copyright © 2021 by Katie Shaw/Arcangel

SIMON PULSE and colophon are registered trademarks of Simon & Schuster, Inc.

For information about special discounts for bulk purchases, please contact Simon & Schuster Special Sales at 1-866-506-1949 or business@simonandschuster.com.

The Simon & Schuster Speakers Bureau can bring authors to your live event. For more information or to book an event contact the Simon & Schuster Speakers Bureau at 1-866-248-3049 or visit our website at www.simonspeakers.com.

Cover designed by Jess LaGreca

Interior designed by Mike Rosamilia

The text of this book was set in Bembo.

Manufactured in the United States of America

2 4 6 8 10 9 7 5 3 1

This book has been cataloged with the Library of Congress.

ISBN 978-1-5344-8764-2 (trade pbk)

ISBN 978-1-4391-2030-9 (eBook)

For Delaney

One

WHAT DO YOU KNOW ABOUT YOURSELF? WHAT ARE YOUR stories? The ones you tell yourself, and the ones told by others. All of us begin somewhere. Though I suppose the truth is that we begin more than once; we begin many times. Over and over, we start our own tales, compose our own stories, whether our lives are short or long. Until at last all our beginnings come down to just one end, and the tale of who we are is done.

This is the first story I ever heard about myself: that I came into this world before my time. And that my coming was so sudden, hot, and swift, it carried everything before it away, including my mother's life.

Full of confusion was the day of my birth, of portents, and

of omens. Just at daybreak, a flock of white birds flew across the face of the sun. Its rising light stained their wings bloodred. This was an omen of life taking flight.

At full noon, every single tree in every single orchard on my father's estate burst into bloom at once, in spite of the fact that it was October. This was an omen of life's arrival.

At dusk, a great storm arose, catching everyone by surprise. My mother was in her garden, the one she planted and tended with her own two hands, when two claps of thunder, one from the east and the other from the west, met above her head in a great collision of sound. The earth shook beneath her feet. Crying out, my mother tumbled to the ground. What this portended nobody ever did decide, because it was at precisely this moment that I declared my intention to be born.

Fortunately for my mother, she was not alone. The healer, Old Mathilde, was with her, as she often was when my father was away from home. Just how old Old Mathilde is, no one really knows. But no matter what her years, she was strong and hale enough to lift my mother up and carry her indoors—through the gate in the garden wall and around the side of the house, up the steps to the front door, and across the great hall. Then, finally, up a wide set of stairs from the great hall to the second floor. By the time Old Mathilde reached my mother's chamber, it was storming in earnest, and she, herself, was breathing hard. The wind wailed like a banshee. Hailstones clattered against the roof with a sound like military drums.

Old Mathilde set my mother gently on the bed, paused to catch her breath. Then she summoned Susanne, who worked in the kitchen, instructing her to bring hot water and soft towels. But when Mathilde went to stir up the coals, the wind got there first, screaming down the chimney, putting out the fire. Not content to do this in my mother's room alone, the wind then extinguished every other fire throughout my father's great stone house by the sea, until not so much as a candle remained lit. All the servants quaked in fear. The women buried their heads beneath their aprons, and the men behind their arms, for nobody could remember such an event ever occurring before.

And so it was first in shadow, and then in darkness, that Old Mathilde and my mother strove to bring me into the world. Just before midnight, I arrived. At my coming, the storm ceased as suddenly as it had begun. A great silence filled the great stone house. Into it came the loud voice of the sea, and then my mother's quiet voice, asking Old Mathilde to place me in her waiting arms. She asked this just as the clocks throughout the house began to strike midnight: the only hour in all the world that begins in one day and ends in another. This was the moment I knew my mother's touch for the first and only time.

And this is the story Old Mathilde has told me each and every time I asked her to: that, with my green eyes, I gazed up, and with her green eyes, my mother gazed back down. She ran one hand across my head, her fingers lingering on my bright red hair, for this, too, was the exact same shade as her own. Then she bent her head and pressed a kiss upon my brow. I carry the mark of it to this day, the faintest smudge of rose just at my hairline.

"Mathilde," my mother said then, and with the sounding of her own name, Old Mathilde understood what my coming into the world before my time would cost. For she recognized the sound my mother's voice made—a sound that was both less and more than it had ever been before.

No one is better at understanding the world than Old Mathilde, at being able to see things for what they truly are. This is what makes her such a good healer, I suppose. For how can you mend a thing, any thing, if you cannot truly see what is wrong? Some things, of course, cannot be healed, no matter how much you want them to be, no matter how hard you try. Old Mathilde was not a magician. She was simply very good at helping wishes come true.

"Will you hear a wish?" my mother asked now.

Just for an instant, Old Mathilde closed her eyes, as if summoning the strength to hear what would come. For my mother was asking to bestow the most powerful wish there is, one that is a birth and death wish, all at the same time. Then Old Mathilde opened her eyes and gave the only answer she could, also the one that was in her heart.

"I will grant whatever you wish that lies within my power, Constanze, my child."

Constanze d'Este. That was my mother's name.

"I wish for you to be my daughter's godmother," Constanze d'Este replied. "Love her for me, care for her when I am gone, for I fear her father will do neither one. When he looks at her, he will not find joy in the color of her hair and eyes. He will not see the way that I live on. Instead, he will see only that she came too soon, and that her arrival carried me out of this life.

"Besides, he is a man and a great lord. He wished for his first child to be a boy."

"What you wish for is easily granted," Old Mathilde said. "For I have loved this child with all my heart since she was no more than a dream in yours. As for Etienne . . ." Etienne de Brabant. That is my father's name. "I suppose a man may be a great lord and a great fool all at once. What shall I call her, while I'm loving her so much?"

At this point in the story, Old Mathilde always does the same thing: She smiles. Not because the circumstances she's relating are particularly happy, but because smiling is what my mother did.

"Call her by whatever name you think best," she replied. "For you will raise her, not I."

"Then I will give her your name," Old Mathilde said. "For she should have more of her mother than just the color of her hair and eyes, and a memory she is too young to know how to hold."

And so I was named Constanze, after my mother. And no sooner had this been decided, than my mother died. Old

Mathilde sat beside the bed, her eyes seeing the two of us together even in the dark, until my mother's lips turned pale, her arms grew cold, and the clouds outside the window parted to reveal a spangle of high night stars. Not once in all that time, so Old Mathilde has always claimed, did I so much as stir or cry.

When the slim and curving sickle of the moon had reached the top of the window, then begun its slide back down the sky, Old Mathilde got up from her chair and lifted me gently from my mother's arms. She carried me downstairs to the great open fireplace in the kitchen. Holding me in the crook of one arm, she took the longest poker she could find and stirred up the coals.

Not even such a storm as had descended upon us that night could altogether put out the kitchen fire—the fire that is the heart of any house. Once the coals were glowing as they should, Old Mathilde wrapped me in a towel of red flannel, took the largest of our soup kettles down from its peg, tucked me inside it, and nestled the pot among the embers so that I might grow warm once more.

As she did, I began to cry for the very first time. And at this, as if the sound of my voice startled them back into existence, all the other fires throughout the great stone house came back to life. Flurries of sparks shot straight up every chimney, scattering into the air like red-hot fireflies.

In this way, I earned a second name that night, the one that people use and remember, in spite of the fact that the name

Constanze is a perfectly fine one. Nobody has ever called me that, not even Old Mathilde. Instead, she calls me by the name I was given for the coals that kept me warm, for the fires I brought back to life with the sound of my own voice.

Child of cinders. *Cendrillon.*

Two

Two weeks to the day after I was born, my father came home, thundering into the courtyard on a great bay horse ridden so long and hard its coat was white with lather as if covered in sea foam. Where he had been on the night of my birth, where since, are tales that, for many years, would remain untold. But he was often sent far and wide on business for the king, so Old Mathilde sent word of what had happened out from the great stone house knowing that, sooner or later, the news would find my father and bring him home.

Just at the counterpoint to the hour of my birth he came, full noon, when the sun was like an orange in the sky. Around his neck, beneath his cloak, he wore a sling of cloth, and in this sling there was a baby boy. My father pulled the horse up short, tossed the reins to a waiting groom, threw his leg over his horse's neck, and slid to the ground. Even at his journey's end, my father's desire to reach my mother burned so hot and bright that the heels of his boots struck sparks from the courtyard cobblestones. He tossed off his cloak, pulled the sling from around his neck, and thrust it and the burden it carried into Old Mathilde's arms.

"Where is she?" he asked.

"In her garden," Old Mathilde replied.

Without another word, my father took off at a dead run. Around the side of the house, he sped through the gate in the stone wall, and into the place my mother had loved best in all the world, aside from the shelter of my father's arms: the garden she had planted with her own two hands. Surrounded by a high stone wall to protect it from the cold sea winds, it was so cunningly made that it could be seen from only one room inside the house: my mother's own bedchamber, the same room in which I had been born.

Old Mathilde had buried my mother beneath a tree whose blossoms were pale pink in spring, whose leaves turned yellow in the autumn, and whose boughs carried tiny red apples no bigger than a thumbnail all through the winter months. It was the only one like it on all my father's lands. My mother had brought it with her as a sapling on her wedding day as a gift to her new husband, a pledge of their new life. Now the mound of earth which marked her grave was a gentle oblong shape beneath its boughs, as if Constanze d'Este had fallen asleep and some thoughtful servant had come along and covered her with a blanket of soft green grass from her head to her toes.

My father fell to his knees beside my mother's grave, and now a second storm arose, one that needed no interpretation, for all who saw it understood its meaning at once. This storm was nothing less than my father's grief let loose upon the world. His rage at losing the woman that he loved. The trees in the orchards tossed their heads in agony; the clear blue sky darkened overhead, though there was not a single cloud. At the base of the cliffs upon which my father's great stone house sat, the sea hurled itself against the land as if to mirror his torment.

My father threw his head back, fists raised above his head, his mouth stretched open in a great O of pain. But he did not shed a single tear, nor make a single sound. He threw himself across my mother's grave, his fists striking the earth once, twice, three times. As his fists landed for the third and final time, a single bolt of jagged lightning speared down from the cloudless sky. It struck the tree which sheltered my mother's grave, traveled down its trunk, up into all its limbs, killing the tree in an instant, turning the new green grass beneath it as brown as the dust of an August road. At that moment, the storm ceased. And from that day onward, even when every other living thing on my father's lands prospered, on the grave of my mother, Constanze d'Este, not so much as a single blade of grass would thrive.

At last my father got to his feet, turned his back upon my mother's grave, left the garden, and went inside. He climbed the wide stairs, two at a time, until he reached my mother's bedroom door. He pushed it open, slammed it behind him, turned the key in the lock with a sound that echoed upstairs and down. Then, for many hours, there was silence as he stayed in my mother's room alone.

Just as night was falling he emerged, locked the door behind him (from the outside this time), then climbed a thin and winding set of stairs to the very top of the house. There, a stiff sea wind blowing in his face, he threw the key to my mother's room as hard as he could. It was still flying through the air when he turned away, and made the climb back down. All the way to the kitchen and Old Mathilde.

"Show me the infant," my father said, and, in spite of herself, Old Mathilde shivered, for never had she heard a voice so cold. The kind of cold that comes when the heart gives up on itself and abandons hope, a cold no fire on earth could ever warm. But Old Mathilde had not grown old by frightening easily.

"You may see both babes for yourself," she said. "For there they are, together."

And sure enough, in a cradle by the fire—for the soup kettle was not big enough for two, and besides I had outgrown it two whole days ago—the baby boy my father had brought with him from who-knew-where and I were lying, side by side. My hair was as bright as a copper basin; his, as dark as cast

11

iron. My eyes, as bright and as green as fresh asparagus; his, a changeable and tumultuous gray, like the sea beneath the sky of a winter storm. For a time Old Mathilde did not even try to measure, my father stood motionless, gazing down at us both.

"She has the look of her mother," he finally said, and the pain in his voice was as bright as a sword.

Old Mathilde nodded. "That she does."

Etienne de Brabant exhaled one breath, and then another, as if his own body was struggling with itself.

"I should have been here!" he finally burst out. "If I had been with her, things might have been different."

"Some things most certainly would have been," Old Mathilde replied. And now she inhaled one quiet breath of her own, for she knew my father would not like to hear what must follow. "But your presence would not have changed the outcome. Not even I could do that, Etienne. Some things are beyond my power to heal."

My father spun toward her. "Your power!" he exclaimed. "You have none. What good is power if you cannot use it as you wish? You are nothing but a powerless old woman. You let Constanze die."

"Do you think I would not have saved her if I could?" Old Mathilde asked. "If so, then you are wrong. And you forget that every kind of power has its own boundaries, Etienne. That is how you know its strength and its form.

"I cannot summon up things that must not happen. That

which must take place, I cannot stop. All I can do is to help make the wishes that lie between come true. My power must stop at the boundaries of life."

My father began to laugh then, and the sound was bitter and wild. "A wish?" he exclaimed. "Is that what you want? You expect me to bestow a wish upon this child that has robbed me of so much?"

"It is what Constanze would have wanted," Old Mathilde said, "and what she herself did. If you cannot bring yourself to do it yet, try starting with the boy. You must have brought him to me for a reason. Therefore, there must be some wish you would bestow."

But by now, Father was nodding his head in agreement, as if Old Mathilde's words had recalled to his mind a task that he had left undone.

"I wish the boy to be raised as a member of my household," he said. "Give him no special honors, yet treat him fairly and well. But on pain of death, he is never to be permitted to leave my lands, not even when he is grown. Not unless I send for him."

"By what name shall I call him?" Old Mathilde asked.

My father shrugged. "By whatever name that comes to mind. What he is called is not important."

This is sheer nonsense, of course. If what we are called is not important, why bother with a name at all? But Old Mathilde had also not grown old by being stupid. She knew when to hold her tongue and when to speak her mind. She had named one child. She could name another.

"And your daughter?" she asked softly. "You must wish something for her, Etienne. Constanze is dead, and it is your right to grieve for her. But you and your daughter are alive. With every beat your two hearts make, each of you wishes for something, for to wish is to be alive. This is a fact you cannot escape."

"Not even if I wish to?" my father inquired.

"Not even then," Old Mathilde replied.

"Then hear the wish I will bestow upon my daughter," my father said. "I wish that I might never see her again, unless the sight of her can give back the peace that she has stolen. As I imagine that day will never come, matters should work out well."

"Matters often do that," Old Mathilde said. Here she reached to tuck the blanket more securely around me for, at the sound of my father's wish, as if struggling to be free of a burden, I had done my best to kick the blanket aside. "Though rarely in the way that men suppose. Still, you have wished, and I have heard you. I will do my best to see your wish is carried out in its own good time."

My father turned away then. Away from the unnamed baby boy and me and toward the kitchen door. He put his hand upon the latch, then paused.

"I do not think that we will meet again, Mathilde," he said.

"For I will never come back to this place, if it lies within my choice."

"I imagine we shall both have to wait and see about that," Old Mathilde answered, her voice ever so slightly tart. "I cannot see the future any more than you can, Etienne. The difference is, I am content in this, and you are not."

"I will never be content again," my father said. "Not in this, or in anything else."

He lifted the latch, pushed open the door, and stepped out into the world without looking back, letting the door swing closed behind him. That was the last anyone in the great stone house saw of him for a very long time.

Three

AND SO WE GREW UP TOGETHER, THE BOY WHOSE FIRST beginning nobody knew, and the girl who came into the world before her time. Old Mathilde named him Raoul, and it was easy enough to figure out why. More often than not he reminded us all of a grumpy bear, so it seemed only right that he should have a name to go along with it, one that sounded like a growl.

Not that he was mean-spirited, for he was not. It was more that there was never a moment, except, perhaps, for when he slept, that Raoul did not carry the mystery of his beginning like a burden on his back, a mark upon his soul. Even I knew more about myself than he did, never mind that most of what I knew was painful. Sometimes it is better to know an unpleasant thing than nothing at all.

We made quite a pair together as we grew. But then we always had, from the moment Old Mathilde first placed us side by side. Raoul with his dark, storm-cloud looks, I with my bright ones, the sun coming out from behind the cloud. I cannot claim that this meant I was always good-natured. My temper could run as hot as the color of my hair, and come on as suddenly as my unexpected entrance into the world. But I always spoke my feelings, right out plain, while Raoul often held his inside and left them to smolder.

Old Mathilde honored the wish my father had made the night of Raoul's arrival. He was always treated fairly and well, no differently from any of the rest of us, including me. I might be the daughter of the lord of the house, but nobody paid much attention to that fact. My father had made it quite clear he didn't want me. I was hardly in any position to pull rank, even if that had been the way my nature was inclined. Besides, nobody who lived in Etienne de Brabant's great stone house by the sea had any time to put on airs. We were too busy working to stay alive.

The lands of my father's estate were beautiful and fertile. But, as if the lightning bolt that struck my mother's grave had somehow planted the seed of my father's unrest within our soil, what our fields and orchards might yield could never quite be predicted ahead of time.

17

One year, every single squash plant grew tomatoes. We made sauce until our hands turned red, then carried our jars to the closest town on market days to barter for what our fields had been unwilling to provide.

Some years our apple trees actually gave us apples. But their limbs were just as likely to be weighed down by cherries or plums. For three years running we had pears instead, followed by three straight years of oranges, a fruit which had never been known to grow so close to the sea before. After that, things seemed to settle down, as if the earth and what my father had called down to strike it had reached some sort of truce. How long it would last, only time itself would show.

And then there was the great stone house itself: huge, drafty, gorgeous. Rising straight up from the center of a great sheer cliff of stone so pale you could see your hand through it on a piece cut thin enough. Even in the darkest hours of the darkest night, the house seemed to give off its own faint glow. Veins of color ran through it, red and green, and a gray that turned to shimmering silver just as the sun went down. One bank of windows faced outward, toward the sea. A second, back toward the land that sustained us.

We were not an easy place to sneak up on.

This was fortunate since, for as long as even the oldest among us can remember, even on the brightest and sunniest of days, the country of my birth has lived under the shadow of war. In most ways, and on most days, we look like everybody else.

We get up in the morning, wash our faces, put on our everyday clothes. We till our fields, bake our bread, take afternoon naps with our cats or dogs when the sun grows too hot to work outdoors.

But even as we sleep, we have one eye open, one ear cocked, to discover if trouble is coming, carried on the back of the sea, or stirring up dust as it marches down the road. The desire for peace fills our hands with purpose during the day; the fear of war haunts our dreams at night.

There is one place, one land, we fear most of all. A place we do not even name aloud, for to do so is considered bad luck, as good as a summons for disaster to arrive. It lies two days' hard riding on horseback to the north of the great stone house. One day's sailing if the wind is right.

Some say our conflict is only natural. That those with common borders always fight. Others, that it is personal, the result of an incident so bitter and terrible, to speak it aloud is as good as shedding blood. I do not know the truth of things, myself. But I do know this much: We watch the sea in the great stone house. For there is a prophecy that proclaims it is the sea that will carry our salvation, or our doom. In the helpful way that prophecies sometimes have, it further proclaims it may be difficult to tell the two apart.

So I kept my eyes on the sea one autumn afternoon, the day before I turned sixteen. I squinted a little beneath the brim of my straw hat as I worked my way down the first row of the

19

pumpkin patch, for the day was crisp and fine, and the sunlight on the water quick and bright. I was hoeing weeds, trying, without much success, not to think about what might happen when my birthday actually arrived. For on that day, as was traditional, I would make the second most powerful kind of wish there is: the one you speak silently, to your own heart alone, on each and every anniversary of the day that you were born.

For at least ten years now, my wish had been the same: that something I planted on my mother's grave might thrive.

Over the years I had tried many different things. Pansies that showed their brave faces through even our bleakest winters. Scarlet runner beans. Bee balm. Several times I had coaxed what I had planted into reluctant life, but none of them had ever thrived. No matter what I planted, no matter when I planted it, when I went to my mother's grave on the morning of my birthday, it was always to discover that every single thing I planted there had died.

It had absolutely nothing to do with the weather; of this I was certain. Nothing to do with what happened above the ground. It was what lay beneath that doomed my efforts to failure, year after year, time after time. There, the rage and grief my father had called down into our lands still held on and would not let go.

I reached the end of the row of pumpkins, reversed direction, my back now facing the sea, and started up the row beside it. The pumpkin patch was in the farthest corner of the kitchen garden, at the very edge of the great cliff on which the great stone house sat. If I went too far, I could tumble straight off the land and into the ocean.

I jabbed the hoe downward, slicing through the roots of a thistle. *This year will be different,* I thought. Tomorrow morning, I would awaken to find that what I had planted on my mother's grave was still alive and well. Because finally, I had chosen a plant so sturdy and obvious, it was literally staring me in the face: pumpkins.

Out of all the things that grew on our lands, the pumpkins were the most reliable. Though you might plant one variety and end up with another, you always got some sort of pumpkin. This year, we had the most abundant crop any of us had ever seen. Fat ones and tall ones, small ones and large. Pumpkins with skin as pale as ghosts growing alongside those with skin as vivid as orange rinds.

But the most beautiful ones of all were the ones I'd planted on my mother's grave. They'd come up almost at once, producing great curling vines. The pumpkins were squat and fat, as if, each night, a family of well-fed raccoons had snuck into the beds and sat upon them. Their skin was an orange as bright as newly polished copper. Thick ribs curved down their bodies from top to bottom, some as wide across as my forearm. Surely pumpkins as bright and sumptuous as these would still be alive tomorrow morning. And if they were, then my wish had come true. I would have broken the curse my father's grief had laid upon us.

In which case, I would need to make an entirely new wish.

The only problem was, I didn't have the faintest idea what it should be.

"You're thinking about tomorrow, aren't you?" Raoul's voice suddenly broke into my thoughts. I realized that I was standing with the hoe straight out in front of me, extending into the air. I brought it back to earth with a *thump*.

"How could you tell?" I inquired dryly.

Raoul smiled. "I think it was the angle of the hoe," he answered. He cocked his head. "Aren't your arms tired?"

"As a matter of fact, they are," I said, and at this, he laughed aloud. Raoul hardly ever laughs. It's simply not the way he's made. As if to make up for behaving in a fashion totally unlike his usual self, he snatched the hoe from my hands, elbowed me aside, and began to work on the weeds himself.

"Why is it that a good crop of anything always brings a good crop of weeds as well?" he inquired after a moment.

I gave a snort. "Please," I said. "Remember where you are." We continued moving along the row in silence for a moment. "Have you made up your mind what to wish for tomorrow?"

"The same thing as always," Raoul replied. He made the hoe bite deep, pulled it back with a jerk. All trace of laughter was gone from him now. "Unless some traveling storyteller arrives to tell the tale of my birth between now and midnight."

Raoul had wished for the same thing every year too: to know who he truly was, the beginnings of his story.

"I'm sorry," I said suddenly. "It was a thoughtless question. Give me back the hoe, Raoul. This is my job, not yours."

I reached to tug it from his hands. Raoul held on tight. "Leave it alone, why don't you? It's not a thoughtless question. It's a perfectly sensible one. It just should have been mine, not yours. You're the one whose wish is about to come true."

"It's not tomorrow yet," I replied. "Now give that to me. You're doing it all wrong."

"All I'm doing is killing weeds, Rilla," Raoul said, using the nickname he'd bestowed upon me when we were both small. But he relinquished the hoe. I worked my way to the end of the row, started down the next one. Raoul kept pace beside me. We were facing the sea once more.

"Do you remember the first year we made wishes?" Raoul asked.

"I remember being tempted to wish you would go back to wherever you came from," I replied with a smile. "Old Mathilde gave you every single day of the year from which to choose a birthday, and you selected the same day as mine."

"It wasn't so unreasonable," Raoul protested. "We're so close in age we might have been born on the same day, for all anyone knows."

I gave a snort. We had been over this before. Ever since Raoul had first announced he intended to muscle in on my birthday, we had bickered with each other about it. Some years with good nature, other years not.

"That's not the reason you did it, and you know it," I said.

"No," Raoul replied. "It's not."

I stopped hoeing, on purpose this time. "Then why?" In all the years we had teased each other, we'd never quite gotten down to the reason for his choice.

Raoul dug the dirt with his toe. "It's simple enough," he said. "So simple I would have thought you'd have figured it out by now. You had everything else I wanted, so I thought I might as well have your birthday, as well."

I let the head of the hoe fall to the earth with a *whump*. "What do you mean I had everything you wanted?" I asked.

"Have," Raoul corrected. "Not much has changed, not even in ten years." He moved his arm in a great sweep, as if to take in everything around us. "You have all this. You know who you are and where you come from. You have a home."

"This is as much your home as it is mine," I said, genuinely unsettled now. "Besides, I'm not so sure knowing who I am and where I come from makes me any happier than you are. It's not a very nice feeling to know your father blames you for your mother's death and plans to never forgive you for it."

"At least you know who he is," Raoul answered. "His name, and the name of your mother. It's more than I know."

"But don't you see?" I asked. "The fact that you don't means that you can hope. You could be anyone, Raoul. Your possibilities are endless, while mine are already sewn up tight. And even

24

if you never find out, you'll still be whatever you can make of yourself."

Raoul made a slightly rude sound. "You sound just like Old Mathilde."

I made a face. "I do, don't I? I suppose it could be worse. She's right more than half the time."

"Actually, I think it's more like three quarters," Raoul replied. "That doesn't make this any easier, Rilla."

I put a hand upon his arm. "I know," I said softly.

Raoul reached up, put his hand on top of mine. Even in the depths of winter, Raoul's hands are always warm. I think it's because of all the fires he keeps, banked down, inside himself. He gave my fingers a squeeze, then let his hand drop away. I picked up the hoe, ready to get back to work.

"Rilla," he said suddenly. "Look up."

Before me stretched the great blue arm of the ocean. The surface of the water flashed like fire. I sucked in a breath. Beneath the brim of my sunhat, I lifted a hand to shield my eyes.

"What is that?" I asked, and I could hear the urgency in my own voice now. "Something's not right. The sea glitters like—"

"Like metal," Raoul's voice cut across mine.

I let the hoe slip through my fingers then, never heard it hit the ground. I could think of just one reason for the sea to do that.

"Soldiers," I said. "Armor. How many ships are there, can you tell?" I could not, for my eyes had begun to water.

Raoul took my hand in his, then our feet stumbled in our haste as he tugged me to the end of the row. Half a dozen more paces and we could have jumped right off the edge of the land.

"Seven," he said. "Five hulks and two galleons."

"Five hulks," I whispered, and just speaking the words aloud brought a chill to my heart.

Though the double-decked galleons with their glorious sails were the undisputed masters of the sea, it was the ungainly, flat-bottom hulks with no sails at all we feared the most. These were the ships that could bring the greatest number of soldiers to our shores. Five may not seem like such a great number to you, but the ships were large and our land was small. And there had been no soldiers for nearly twenty years now.

"What flag are they flying, can you see?" I asked, as I dashed a hand across my cheeks in annoyance, hoping to clear the water from my eyes. *Maybe they're not coming for us at all,* I thought. *Perhaps they're going somewhere else. Somewhere far away.*

Raoul was silent for one long moment. "A white flag," he said at last. "In the center, a black swan with a red rose in its beak, and a border of golden thorns."

"No," I whispered, as the earth seemed to sway beneath my feet, for this was the one we feared most of all. One not seen in our land since before I was born, since the marriage of our king and queen had taken place to put an end to bloodshed. "No."

"I can see it clear as day, Rilla," Raoul said, and I took no offense at the sting in his voice. I knew all too well that it was not for me.

"Will they try to land here, do you think?"

Raoul shook his head. "We are not important enough a place, and our shore has too many rocks. They will make for the capital, the court, and go farther down the coast."

"I wish all this would stop," I exclaimed fiercely, the words out of my mouth in the exact same moment I thought them. "I wish that I could find a way to stop it."

This is the third most powerful kind of wish there is: the one you make unbidden, not to your heart, but from it. Only knowing what it is you wish for as you hear own voice, proclaiming it aloud.

No sooner did I finish speaking, than I felt the wind shift, blowing straight into my face, tickling the long braids I wore tucked up beneath my sun hat, then tugging at them hard enough to make the hat fly back. With a quick, hard jerk, the leather chin strap pulled tight against my throat.

"So do I," Raoul said softly.

At his words, the air went perfectly still. Raoul and I stood together, hardly daring to breathe. Then, ever so slowly, the wind began to shift again. Its force became strong, picking up until my skirts streamed straight out to the left, flapping against my legs. Below us, the surface of the water was covered with white-caps. Galleons and hulks alike bucked like unbroken horses.

"The wind is blowing backward," Raoul said, his voice strange.

"It can't do that," I answered. "It never blows in that direction off our coast, not even when it storms."

"I know it," Raoul said. "But it's blowing in that direction now. We wished to find a way to make the fighting stop, and now the wind is blowing backward. We did that. Did we do that?"

"I don't know. But I think we should get out of the wind. It has an unhealthy sound."

"Old Mathilde will know what to do," Raoul said.

Hand in hand, pumpkins and weeds both forgotten, we turned, and raced for the great stone house.

Four

By the time Raoul and I reached the house, Mathilde was gathering each and every living thing and shooing it inside. The rabbits were put into their hutches, the chickens onto their nests, the dogs summoned from the courtyard. Being out in such a wind could do strange things to living beings, Old Mathilde called over its unnatural voice. The wind blowing backward can make you forget yourself.

Once we were all safely indoors, I worked with Old Mathilde and Susanne, who ran the kitchen, to make a fine dinner of chowder and cornbread from the last of our fresh ears of corn. All the rest had already been dried, in preparation for the winter. By the time the meal was ready, the sun was setting. We gathered around the great trestle table in the kitchen for supper—all but Raoul, who took his out to the stables, announcing his intention to stay with the horses until the wind died down.

As if to make up for the fact that he was not always comfortable with people, Raoul was good with animals of all kinds. Perhaps because it had been a horse which had carried him to us in the first place, he loved the horses best of all.

Well into the night the wind blew, until I longed to stuff cotton into my ears to shut out the sound. None of us went to bed. Instead, we stayed in the kitchen, our chairs arranged in a semicircle around the kitchen fire. Old Mathilde worked on her knitting, her needles flashing in the light of the coals. Susanne polished the silver, as if there might yet come a day when someone would arrive who would want to use it. Her daughter, Charlotte, darned socks. Joseph and Robert, the father and son who helped with the orchards and grounds, mended rope. I sorted seeds for next year's planting, wondering what might actually come up.

The clocks struck ten, and then eleven, and still we heard the wind's voice. As the hands of the clock inched up toward midnight, a great tension seemed to fill the kitchen, causing all the air to back up inside our lungs. Midnight is an important hour in general, but it was considered particularly significant in our house. But it was only as the clock actually began to count up to midnight, *one, two, three, four,* that I remembered what the voice of the wind blowing in the wrong direction had pushed to the back of my mind.

When the clocks finished striking twelve, it would be my birthday, and I would learn whether what I wished had come true or not.

Seven, the clocks chimed on their way to midnight. *Eight. Nine. Ten.* And suddenly, I was praying with all my might, with all my heart. *Please,* I thought. *Let the wind stop. Don't let it blow backward on the day of my birth.*

Eleven, the clocks sang throughout the house. And then, in the heartbeat between that chime and the next, the wind died down.

Old Mathilde lifted her head; the hands on her knitting needles paused. Susanne placed the final piece of silver back into its chest with a soft *clink* of metal. *It is just before midnight,* I thought.

Twelve, the clocks struck. And, in that very moment, the wind returned, passing over us in its usual direction, making a sound like a lullaby.

"Oh, but I am tired," Susanne said, as she gave a great stretch. One by one, the others said their good nights and departed. Within a very few moments, Old Mathilde and I were left alone.

"I should go and get Raoul," I said.

Old Mathilde began to bundle up her knitting. "Raoul is fine. He sleeps in the stable half the time anyway. But you may go and get him, if you like. That way, you can both go together."

"How did you . . . ," I began, but at precisely that instant, Raoul burst through the kitchen door. In one hand, he held the lantern he had taken out to the stable.

"Why are you still just standing there?" he asked. "Are we going or not?"

By way of answer, I dashed across the kitchen and, before Raoul quite realized what I intended, I threw my arms around him, burrowing my face into the column of his throat, holding on for dear life. I felt the way his pulse beat against my cheek, the way his free arm, the one that wasn't busy with the lantern, came up to press me close. We stood together for several seconds, just like that.

We look so different, Raoul and I, but in our hearts, we are so very much alike. The same impatience for what we desire dances through our veins. The same need to have our questions answered, our wishes granted. To understand, to know.

And so Raoul had known what I would want to do, now that the wind was running in its proper direction and the clocks had finished striking twelve. He had known that I would never be able to wait until the sun came up to discover if my birthday wish had been granted after so long. More than this, he had given me the greatest gift he could have bestowed. With one short walk from the stable to the house, he had set his own disappointment aside.

Raoul knew already that his wish had not been granted. He knew no more about who he truly was now than he had a year ago, or than he had on the day my father had first brought him home. But still, he had come to find me, knowing I would want to visit my mother's grave, even in the middle of the night.

During the long hours we had waited in the kitchen, the moon had risen. The cobblestones of the courtyard gleamed like mother of pearl; the great stone house shimmered like an opal in the moonglow. The three of us went across the front, then around the corner and along the side opposite the kitchen garden. At last we reached the end of the house and the beginning of the stone wall, just higher than a tall man's head, that marked the boundaries of my mother's garden. Above our heads, surrounding the moon like a handful of scattered sentinels, the stars burned fierce and blue.

"I am afraid," I said suddenly.

"There is no need to be afraid, my Cendrillon," Old Mathilde replied. "Either what you wish for has come true, or it has not. If it hasn't, you must simply try again. Some things must be wished for many times before they come to us."

"Happy birthday, Raoul," I said, as he pushed the gate open.

"And to you, little Cendrillon."

"I'm not little," I said. "And I bet I can still beat you in a foot race."

And with that, we were off and running. I knew every inch of my mother's garden, even in the dark. The rose bushes, espaliered along its walls, the stands of lilies that bloomed in late summer. The daffodils in the spring, the surprise of autumn crocus. A carpet of chamomile was springy underfoot.

There was mint, pungent and sweet. Oregano, brusque and spicy. In the very center of the garden stretched my mother's grave. The limbs of the blasted tree still raised stiffly above it, a silent testimony to my father's rage and grief. Nobody, not even Old Mathilde, had ever been able to bring themselves to cut it down.

Please, I thought, as I raced forward. *Please* was my word of choice that night. *Please let what I wish for come true.* I reached the edge of the grave, skidded to a stop. A split second later, the light from Raoul's lantern shone down upon the oblong of my mother's grave. I fell to my knees beside it, just as my father had done.

"No," I cried out. "No, no, *no!*"

The vines I had planted were still there, and so were the gorgeous orange pumpkins. But now the vines were withered, as if a killing frost had wrapped its icy fingers around them. The pumpkins were split open. Inside, their flesh was black, the pale white seeds gleaming like fragments of bone. From the moment they had come up, all the while that they had grown, their beautiful outsides had all been concealing the very same thing: Inside, they were festering and rotten.

"I can't do it. I won't ever be able to do it, will I?" I sobbed. "He hates me too much. What can grow amid so much hate?"

"Just one thing," Old Mathilde answered quietly. "Only love."

"*Love!*" I cried. I flung myself forward then, onto the grave, digging my fingers deep into the flesh of the nearest pumpkin. I brought my hands back up, dripping and disgusting. A great stench filled the air, one of unwholesome things kept in the dark too long.

"This," I said, as I flung the first handful from me with all my might. I scooped up more, flung it away, in a desperate frenzy now. "This and this. This is what my father thinks of me. It has nothing to do with love."

"All the more reason that what you wish for should, then," Old Mathilde said, and now she knelt down beside me to take my hands in hers, horrible as they were. I jerked back, but she held on tight. "There are two things in the world you must never give up on, my Cendrillon. And those two things are yourself and love."

"Who said anything about giving up?" I said, as I finally managed to snatch my hands away. "I'm not giving up. I'm just tired of wishing for what I can never have, that's all."

"Then wish for something else," Raoul said without heat.

"You make it sound so simple when you know it's not," I said, the words bitter in my mouth. "But since you request it, then this is what I wish. I wish for a mother to love me, a mother for me to love. And perhaps put some sisters into the bargain. Two would be a nice number. That way, perhaps there will be a chance that one of them might actually like me."

"For heaven's sake, Rilla," Raoul exclaimed. "You know you're not supposed to speak a birthday wish aloud."

"What difference does it make?" I flung back. "It's not going to come true anyhow."

"You don't know that for sure," Raoul said. "Now come inside and get cleaned up. You smell disgusting."

"Thank you very much," I said. "For that, you can help me up."

Raoul reached down and pulled me to my feet. But when I expected him to let go, he held on. "I am sorry, Rilla," he said. "You see why I think hope is such a tricky thing?"

"I do." I nodded.

"Come," Old Mathilde said. "I am an old woman, my bones ache, and there will still be chores in the morning. Let us go back inside."

After the others had gone to bed, I stood at the kitchen sink, scrubbing my hands till they were red and raw. But the scent of my father's hate could not be washed entirely away. It clung to my skin, a faint rotten smell. At last, I gave up. I climbed the stairs to my room, curled up in bed, and pressed my face against the windowpane, gazing out at the stars.

One wish, I thought. *That is all I want. Why is that so very much to ask?*

And now I had thrown my birthday wish away. Even worse, I had thrown it away in anger. *You are your father's daughter, after all, Cendrillon,* I thought. *Tonight, you've proved you're no better than he is.*

Like him, I had chosen anger over love.

I began to weep then, great, hot tears. I hate to weep, even when I know I have good cause. It makes me feel like I have failed, as my wish had failed that night.

At last, I put my head upon my pillow and cried myself to sleep, an act I had never performed before. Not even on the night that I was born.

Five

BUT IN THE MORNING, IT WAS NOT JUST CHORES AS USUAL. For in the morning, there was a soldier at the kitchen door.

Susanne had just finished the daily ritual of setting the morning's bread to rise. Now she and Old Mathilde were bustling about together, setting out ingredients for two birthday cakes. I wasn't sure how much stomach I would have for mine. In spite of the fact that I had wept myself into an exhausted sleep, I had not slept well. It seemed to me that my dreams were filled with the cries of desperate men. I had been up at the sun's first light.

"Would you like me to gather eggs?" I offered now. Usually, this was among my least favorite of the daily chores. I could never rid myself of the notion that the hens resent the way we snatch their eggs. Raoul tells me I'm being ridiculous, of course—which irritates me because I know he's right.

"That would be helpful. Thank you, Rilla," Old Mathilde replied. We had not spoken of the events of last night, but I saw the way she looked at me with careful, thoughtful eyes. Not surprisingly, I found this irritating too. All in all, not one of my better mornings, birthday or otherwise.

I took the egg basket down from its hook, tucked it into the crook of my arm.

"Make sure you bundle up," Susanne advised. "It's cold out this morning. You mark my words, we'll have a hard frost before the week is out."

I took my shawl down from its peg, wrapped it around my head and across my chest, then tucked the ends into the waistband of my apron as I reached for the kitchen door. I pulled it open, then faltered backward with a startled yelp. I was staring straight down the length of a sword into a pair of startled, desperate eyes.

Old Mathilde was beside me in a flash. In one hand, she held the longest of the fireplace pokers. I heard a bang from across the courtyard, realized it was the sudden slam of the stable door. And then, over the soldier's shoulder, I saw Raoul running toward me, full tilt. Above his head, he swung a leather lead, making it sing like a whip.

"Raoul, be careful!" I shouted, just as the soldier heard the sound himself and began to spin around. I don't know whether he lost his footing, or whether the legs that had carried him this far now abruptly refused to hold him any longer. But, in the next minute, before Raoul could even reach him, the soldier went down. Toppling over like a storm-felled tree, his head struck hard against the cobblestones. Raoul skidded to a stop even as Old Mathilde thrust the fireplace poker into my arms, then elbowed me aside to hurry down the two steps from the kitchen to the courtyard. She knelt beside the stranger, placed her fingers against his neck.

"He lives," she said shortly. "Help me get him into the house."

"Wait a minute," Raoul exclaimed. "You're going to take him in?"

"I took you in," Old Mathilde replied.

"But—" Raoul began.

Old Mathilde straightened up, and looked Raoul right in the eye. "If we treat him like an enemy, that's all he'll ever be," she said. She turned around to look at me in the open kitchen door, where I still stood, hesitating. The expression in her eyes made up my mind. I set the poker aside, put aside the egg basket, and walked down the steps to join her.

"For pity's sake, Rilla," Raoul protested.

"For pity's sake," I said. "That's absolutely right. We wished for the fighting to stop, Raoul. You wished it just as hard as I did." I knelt at the soldier's feet, saw, with horror, that his boots were cut to ribbons, his feet bleeding and torn. "This is our chance to do something more than wish. Now come and help us get him into the house."

Raoul swore then, a thing he almost never does. But even as he did so, he was moving toward Old Mathilde and me, scooting her aside to slip his hands beneath the soldier's shoulders and so take the heaviest part of the body himself.

"I really hope you're right about this," he said. "On three." He counted out, and when he hit the number three, the three of us lifted the soldier from the cobblestones. By the time we made it up the kitchen stairs, Susanne had dragged the cot out and placed it near the fire. We settled the soldier onto it. Then Raoul and I stepped back as Old Mathilde set about discovering the full extent of his injuries.

"Go ahead and fetch those eggs, Cendrillon," she instructed. "You go along with her, Raoul."

"Even if we did the right thing," Raoul murmured, as we made our way to the henhouse, "I reserve the right to say *I told you so* if anything goes wrong."

The soldier ran a fever for a solid week, after which time he was so weak he could hardly hold up his head. His hands had been as torn and bloody as his feet. His clothing had been icy and soaked, as if he had been tossed into the sea, thrown ashore, then been so desperate to get away from the water he had not even bothered to look for a path, but simply climbed straight up the cliff to reach our kitchen door.

Old Mathilde, Susanne, and I took turns caring for him, changing the dressings on his wounded hands and feet, keeping an eye on him while he slept, ladling chicken broth down his throat when he awoke. The day he announced he feared he was sprouting feathers was the day we knew he would recover. That was the day he graduated from the cot to a chair.

It was also the day he told us who he was.

His name was Niccolo Schiavone, a minor nobleman's youngest son, born and raised in the land we did not name. He was only about a year older than Raoul and I, and not a soldier, in spite of the sword. He had taken it from the body of a dead comrade in a moment of desperation, certain he would not meet with a shred of kindness upon our shores. The voyage on which he had embarked was his first at sea, his first outside his homeland. He had been sent as a courier, carrying information to the queen herself.

"What kind of message requires warships to send it?" Raoul demanded one night after several weeks had gone by.

Raoul, Old Mathilde, Niccolo, and I were sitting together in the kitchen. During Niccolo's recovery, the days had slid from October into November. It was full winter now. The sea outside our windows was gray, a mirror of the dull and glowering sky; the wind blew hard and cold. But at least it was still blowing in its usual direction. As Niccolo had grown stronger, he had begun to demonstrate his gratitude for the fact that we had rescued him by performing various tasks around the great stone house.

His first feat had impressed us all, but particularly Susanne, and it was this: He revealed his ability to chop onions without crying. Then he graduated to meat, and finally to wood for the kitchen fire, great piles of which were now stacked neatly outside the kitchen door. He re-caned Susanne's rocking chair. When Old Mathilde discovered he had a talent for drawing, she set him to work making sketches of new and bigger cold frames to use in the spring. We had all carefully refrained from mentioning the reason Niccolo was available to perform these tasks in the first place: He had as good as been part of an invasion force.

But the subject of Niccolo's message could not be put off forever, and it was probably inevitable that it would be Raoul who finally brought it up. He might have gone from believing Niccolo intended to murder us all in our beds to grudging acceptance, but he was still a long way from trust. In this, though I don't think either of them realized it, he was no different from Niccolo himself.

"I think that I must give you a true answer," he finally said in response to Raoul's question. "Though there are many in my land who would say that I should not.

"The news I was bringing to the queen is this: Her father is dead. Her brother now sits upon their country's throne. For twenty long years, brother and sister have waited for this moment. Now that their father is dead, his will can no longer hold them back from what it is that they desire: a return to the ways of war."

43

"But why?" I cried. "Why did our two countries ever start fighting in the first place? Do you know?"

Niccolo's dark eyebrows rose, and I could tell that I had taken him completely by surprise.

"Of course I know," he said. "Or I suppose, in fairness, I should say I know what I've been told." He paused for a moment, gazing at each of the three of us in turn. "You truly do not know?"

"We do not speak of it," Raoul said softly. "We do not even name the place you live aloud, for to do so is considered as good as inviting your soldiers to march down our roads."

"Please, Niccolo," I said. "Tell us what you know."

Niccolo rubbed a hand across his face. "To speak the truth," he said, "there isn't all that much to tell. In the land of my birth it is simply said that the conflict between our peoples began with a wish for love, ended in hate, and that in between run rivers of blood. Only when true love can find the way to heal hate's wounds can there be a genuine peace between us once more.

"It is for this reason that our late king married his only daughter to the son of his greatest foe. He hoped that love might grow between them and so put an end to the seemingly endless cycle of war."

"Well, that certainly didn't happen," Raoul said with a snort. "We may have stopped fighting for the time being, but everybody knows that what our king and queen feel for each other is a far cry from love. We're about as far away from court as we can be in this place, and even here we hear rumors of the queen's constant plotting.

"They say it has divided the court. The king has food tasters, to make sure he isn't poisoned. Soldiers sleep at the foot of his bed, and outside his chamber door. And he sends Prince Pascal away from court for months at a time. It's the only way to keep him safe, and from becoming his mother's pawn. They say she will never be satisfied until the first son of her heart and blood sits on the throne."

"Which makes no sense at all," I said. "For Prince Pascal is an only child. Of course he will inherit the throne. All the queen has to do is to wait."

"And the longer she waits," Niccolo said. "The older her son will become. Your king is young, still in his prime. He should live for many years yet. Years which will see his son grow to full manhood. The queen's chance for influence diminishes with every year that goes by. But if her husband were to be killed in battle, and her son came to the throne before he turned eighteen . . ."

"Then he would need a regent," I said. "Someone to help guide him, and who better than his loving mother?"

Niccolo nodded. "That is so."

"So the ships we saw were what they appeared to be," Raoul said. "An invasion fleet. Now that they are destroyed, what will your new king do?"

Niccolo shook his head. "I do not know."

"And you," I said quietly. "What will you do?"

"I have been thinking about that," Niccolo answered slowly. "Much as I might wish to stay here, I don't think I have a choice. I was charged with bringing the queen news of her father's death. I must carry out my charge."

"Someone else has probably brought the queen the news you carry by now," Raoul said. "You've been here almost a month."

"True enough," Niccolo acknowledged. "But I have a duty to perform. Ignoring it would bring dishonor to me, and to my family. They probably think I'm dead by now. If for no other reason, I should go to court to send them word I'm still alive."

"When will you go?" I asked.

Niccolo rubbed a hand across his face for a second time. "There's no real reason to put it off," he said. "I could go as early as tomorrow."

"It's a long walk from here to the capital," Raoul observed, but I caught the flicker of a smile. During the days of Niccolo's recovery, a genuine affection had sprung up between the three of us in spite of our initial mistrust.

"Oh, Raoul, for heaven's sake," I exclaimed. "You know better than to pay attention to him when he talks like that, don't you?" I asked Niccolo. "He knows perfectly well we will loan you a horse."

"*Give* is more like it," Raoul replied more somberly. "Even if Niccolo wants to come back, he's not likely to be able to, once he gets to court. He'll be set to carrying messages for someone else. Either that, or be sent back home."

"Why don't you come with me, to ensure the horse's safe return?" Niccolo proposed. "It would be good to have a companion on my journey."

Raoul's face flushed. He stood up so abruptly the stool on which he had been sitting toppled over with a crash. "I thank you, but no. Speaking of horses, it's time for me to see to them. Good night."

He turned and went out without another word, cold air swirling through the room as he opened and closed the door.

"Well," Niccolo said, after a moment. "It's pretty clear I said something wrong. Either of you care to tell me what?"

"Raoul is forbidden to leave de Brabant lands," I said, as I stood to right the upturned stool. "By order of Etienne de Brabant himself."

"De Brabant lands," Niccolo echoed, and I turned toward him at the astonishment in his voice. "These lands belong to Etienne de Brabant?"

"They do," I acknowledged.

Niccolo clapped his hands together, like a child who had just solved a knotty puzzle. "Oh, but surely this explains everything," he cried. "Why did you not speak of this before?"

"It didn't occur to me it was important," I said. I shot a glance in Old Mathilde's direction. "I'm not sure I understand why it is now."

"It explains why you would take me in and nurse me back to health where others would only see an enemy," Niccolo replied. "Etienne de Brabant supports the queen. He is the leader of her faction at court. If these are de Brabant lands, surely you, too, must be sympathetic to her cause."

"We wish for our two countries to be at peace," Old Mathilde said, when it became clear that I could not speak at all. I had never heard of any of this before. "Nothing less, and nothing more. We have no time to concern ourselves with court intrigues in a place such as this."

Niccolo's face clouded. "I'm sorry," he said. "I didn't mean—"

"Why?" I burst out.

Niccolo turned back to me, the confusion he was feeling clear upon his face. "Why what?"

"Why does Etienne de Brabant support the queen's cause?"

"I don't know the details," Niccolo admitted. "For it happened many years ago. He was loyal to the king, or so they say, until some service he performed while in the king's service brought him endless sorrow. After that, he turned his back on all that he had been before. He has been the queen's man ever since."

"Ever since," I echoed quietly, though my heart was thundering in my ears like a kettle drum. I turned my head, and met Old Mathilde's eyes. "Since the day he received word of my mother's death," I said. "Since the day that I was born. That's the day his endless sorrow began, don't you think?"

Niccolo jerked, as if Old Mathilde had jabbed him with one of her knitting needles.

"Wait a minute," he exclaimed. "You're saying you are Etienne de Brabant's daughter? I did not know he had a child!"

"I am the child of Etienne de Brabant and Constanze d'Este," I said. "My mother died the night that I was born, while my father was far from home, on the king's business, or so it now seems. My father does not forgive, nor does he forget, what happened the night that I was born. That's why you've never heard of me. My father does his best to pretend I don't exist."

"Then he is a fool," Niccolo said. "For you are a daughter of which any father would be proud."

I felt the blood rush to my face, the sudden stab of tears at the backs of my eyes.

"It is kind of you to say so," I said. "But I—"

Old Mathilde got to her feet, dropping her knitting into her basket with a rustling sound.

"We have had enough of questions and answers for tonight, I think," she said in a firm yet quiet voice. "You will need a good night's sleep, Niccolo, if you truly intend to go tomorrow morning. It's a long journey. You should start at first light."

Niccolo stood up in response to her words, but I felt the way his eyes stayed on my face. "You are right," he said. "I will say good night. But I . . ." He paused and took a breath. "I would be sorry to think any words of mine had caused unhappiness," he went on. "Particularly after all your care."

"They haven't," I said. "You took me by surprise, that's all. Good night."

"Good night," he said.

The kitchen was silent for many moments after he had gone.

"It's too bad Raoul can't go with him," I remarked at last. "They would make a good pair."

"Indeed they would," Old Mathilde replied. "Perhaps they will get their chance yet."

"What do you wish for, Mathilde?" I suddenly inquired.

"That the wishes of those I love come true," she replied. "No more questions now. It's time for bed."

Six

THAT WINTER WAS THE COLDEST ANY OF US COULD RECALL. The ground froze solid, though we had no snow. Day after day, the sea outside our windows churned like an angry cauldron. If you put your bare hand on the outside of the house, you could burn the skin on your fingers, it was so cold. The only thing that never seemed to change was the surface of my mother's grave. It was as bare and brown as always.

December came and went, and then January. In February, the clear cold abruptly loosed its grasp. The sky filled with clouds and the rains came down, swelling the rivers with water, choking the lanes with mud. Then, one morning, beneath the bare branches of the rosebushes in my mother's garden, I saw that the tenacious green shoots of snowbells were beginning to push their way up through the waterlogged soil. The wood hyacinths in the orchards were right behind them. The first flowers bloomed on the first day of March.

On the second day, Niccolo came back to the great stone house.

He rode into the courtyard in the strange and beautiful gleam of twilight, just as the sun came out from behind a cloud. Its rays struck the house, lighting up all the colors within the pale white stone. I was in my mother's garden, trying to prune the last of the rosebushes before the light expired. I saw the way the house abruptly blazed with color, heard the clatter of horses' hooves, Raoul's shout. And then I was up and running, pushing the gate from the garden open with both hands, dashing along the side of the house and into the courtyard.

Niccolo was still on horseback, on the sleek dappled gray that had been Raoul's choice. Raoul had one hand in the horse's mane, the other on Niccolo's leg as it gripped the horse's flank. As I rounded the corner, the horse lowered his head and pushed against Raoul's chest, hard enough to knock him back five whole steps.

"He is glad to see you," I heard Niccolo say. "He's been doing his best to pull my arms from my sockets ever since we sighted the house."

"It's on top of a hill," Raoul said. "You can see it for miles."

Niccolo laughed. "Believe me, I know." He saw me then. "Cendrillon!"

He tossed the reins to Raoul, slid from the horse's back, and crossed the courtyard with quick and eager strides to twirl me around in a great rambunctious hug. The kerchief I wore upon my head spun loose and my braids went flying.

"I am glad to see you," he said.

"And I you," I replied. "Welcome home."

"I have seen all the beauties of the court," Niccolo went on, as he set me on my feet. "Not a single one of them can compare to you."

"Oh, ho," Raoul said with a laugh from where he still stood beside the horse. "He has come back to us a silver-tongued courtier. You had best watch your step around him, Cendrillon."

I retrieved my kerchief, bound my hair back up. Unbraided and brushed out, my hair falls almost to my knees, but I always keep it covered. Loose hair only gets in the way when I'm working, and I have never quite forgotten the day, when I was twelve and beginning to feel the first stirrings of vanity, that Raoul claimed its color was so bright it kept the villagers awake at night.

"So," I heard Old Mathilde's voice say. "The traveler has come home."

"And I bring news," Niccolo said, his expression sobering. "News I must share quickly, for there isn't much time. Etienne de Brabant is married again. His new wife and daughters follow close behind me."

"Married!" I exclaimed. I put a hand out, as the world began to whirl, and felt Niccolo's hand grasp mine. "My father is married? When did this happen?"

"Just last week," Niccolo said. "Chantal de Saint-Andre is your stepmother's name. She is a wealthy widow, and a ward of the crown. None may marry her but by the king's command."

"And now the king has married her to my father?" I said. I knew I sounded stupid, but I could not seem to get my brain to function. "But why?"

"That," Niccolo said succinctly, "is the question to which all the court would like an answer. Your new stepmother and stepsisters most of all."

"Stepsisters!" I cried. "I have stepsisters?"

"Two," Niccolo answered. "Their names are Amelie and Anastasia."

"I think," I said faintly, "that I would like to sit down." In fury and desperation, I had wished for a mother and two sisters. And now my father was married, and his wife and two step-daughters were on their way to my door.

"I can't tell you more. I'm sorry," Niccolo said. "I'm afraid there isn't time. They should be here any minute. I only rode on ahead to try to give you some warning."

"Why did you bring them?" I asked. "Do you serve my father now?"

"Because I was convenient," Niccolo answered. "I knew the way, and besides—"

"You are from the queen's home country," I filled in. "No matter what the king commands my father to do, you may be relied upon to keep the queen's interests in mind."

"Something like that," Niccolo acknowledged. "Cendrillon, there is one other thing that you should know."

But before he could finish, there was a great clatter of hooves as a coach swept into our courtyard. The spokes of its wheels were coated in mud; great spatters of it rose halfway up the doors and sides. Even the coachman was covered in the huge clumps tossed upward by the horses' hooves. He pulled back hard on the reins and brought the two broad-backed horses to a halt at the bottom of the steps that led to our front door. Their hot breath steamed in the air; curls of steam rose up from their backs and flanks.

Niccolo released my hand, and moved toward the coach at once. Raoul stayed beside the dappled gray. Old Mathilde made a gesture, and together we moved to stand at the top of the steps, a welcoming committee of two women, one young, one old. That would be all Etienne de Brabant's house could offer his new wife and daughters. Mathilde pulled one of my arms through hers, tucking my fingers into the crook of her elbow. I held on for dear life.

Carefully, so as not to tumble fresh mud on the occupants inside, Niccolo opened the coach door. He unfolded the steps, then extended one hand, his body bent at the waist in a bow. And it was only at this moment that I truly understood what should have been obvious to me at once: My new step-mother was of noble birth. She and her daughters would be unlike anything the great stone house had seen in a good long time.

I wonder if they will have seen anything quite like us, I thought. And then I ceased to think at all. For just then, a hand emerged from inside the carriage, its fingers encased in a supple leather glove. It grasped Niccolo's, held on tightly, then was followed by the rest of the arm. A head emerged, neck bent down so as not to knock the top of it against the inside of the door. Next, a pair of shoulders, wrapped in a dark blue cloak. And now, finally, one foot was upon the carriage steps and the woman inside the coach was straightening up. At this, my mind came flowing back.

Oh, but she is so beautiful, I thought.

My stepmother's skin was as pale as our best porcelain dishes. Peeking out from beneath the hood of her cloak, her hair was midnight dark. Her eyes were the same deep blue as the hood which framed them. At their expression, I felt a strange feeling in my chest, as if a great hand was squeezing it, tight. So tight I couldn't quite get a full breath of air.

So beautiful and so unhappy, I realized. And absolutely deter-mined not to give way to what she felt. Gazing at my new stepmother's face, I had a sudden vision of a stream in early spring, just before the final thaw. On the surface, a thin sheet of ice. But beneath the surface, the current was racing, swift and strong. Where it might carry us, I could not say. Perhaps not even Chantal de Saint-Andre herself could say.

"My lady," Niccolo said, just as my stepmother's foot touched the cobblestones. "Welcome to the end of your long journey, and your new home."

"Thank you, Niccolo," she said, and at the sound of her voice, I felt a shiver move down my spine. There was absolutely no expression in it, no hint of what she might be feeling at all. "You have cared for us well and I am grateful for it."

She cocked her head then, as if she saw something unexpected in his face. "You are happy to be back in this place, I think," she said, her voice warming ever so slightly.

"Lady, I am," Niccolo said. "In this place I found . . . a surprise. I hope that you may do the same."

"I have no doubt I will," my new stepmother replied, and now her voice was dry. I saw her blue eyes sweep up and outward to take in the great stone house. If she thought it beautiful and was surprised by this, she gave no sign. I knew the moment she spotted Old Mathilde and me, for at last Chantal de Saint-Andre's lips curved in something that might have wished to be a smile.

"We have some welcome, I see," she said.

"A small one, as yet," Old Mathilde said, and she descended the steps, her hold on my arm pulling me along beside her. At the bottom of the steps, she stopped and bobbed a curtsy, once again obliging me to follow suit.

"We are not many here, and we had no word of your arrival till Niccolo came to tell us the news himself, just now. Still, we know what we are about. I am Old Mathilde. And this is Cendrillon."

"Cendrillon," my stepmother echoed, and I felt her gaze on me, and me alone, for the very first time. Not unfriendly, but cool and remote. And suddenly I knew the truth, knew what it was that Niccolo had been trying to tell me when the arrival of the carriage had interrupted him. My stepmother had no idea that her new husband had a child of his own. No idea that I was now her stepdaughter.

"I have never heard such a name before," Chantal de Saint-Andre went on.

"I don't think anyone else has it," I somehow managed to reply. *Fool, idiot, nincompoop,* I thought. *Your father has never acknowledged you, not once in all these years. Why did you think he would do so now?*

But still, I felt the pain of his denial slice straight through my heart. In my simple, homespun dress, my stepmother had mistaken me for a serving girl. And who could blame her? When my own father denied me, who was I to tell Chantal de Saint-Andre the truth of who and what I was?

"The villagers say that, because I am called the child of cinders, the fires in our house will always start, and never go out until I give them leave to do so," I went on.

All of a sudden, my stepmother smiled. A real one this time.

"That's the best news I have heard since we set out," she said. "We have been traveling for more hours than I care to count, and all of them cold ones."

"Then you must come inside and warm yourselves at once," Old Mathilde said. "We will have your rooms prepared before you know it."

"Thank you," Chantal de Saint-Andre replied. "I believe that is as warm a welcome as any stranger could wish for."

"Oh, but you are not a stranger anymore, my lady," Old Mathilde said, her voice soft but as unyielding as the stones upon which we stood. "You are now the mistress of this house. I hope you will not mind becoming acquainted with the kitchen first. With so few of us, it's the only place we always keep a fire going."

"The kitchen!" exclaimed a sudden voice. "I most certainly will not!"

And that was the moment I realized that I had been so caught up in my new stepmother that I had let all thoughts of her daughters slip my mind. They were out of the carriage themselves now, standing beside it in the courtyard, bundled in cloaks up to their chins, one forest green, the other a deep and fertile brown. Both had their mother's fine pale skin, her dark and lustrous hair. One had blue eyes, and the other brown ones. The blue-eyed girl was a little taller, more angular than her sister, and I thought her cheeks were flushed with anger rather than with cold.

So you are the one who is not fond of kitchens, I thought.

She stomped her foot against the cobblestones as if she had read my mind.

"I have not traveled for hours in a dark and freezing coach to sit in the kitchen like some serving maid," she proclaimed in a bright, clear voice. "I will stand out here if I have to, until a proper room is prepared. Till then, I will not set a foot inside."

"You'll just be cold longer," the girl beside her said, her voice exasperated but not altogether unkind. "Can you not make things easier instead of more difficult, just this once? It's only a kitchen, Anastasia. It's hardly the end of the world."

"This whole place is the end of the world," the girl named Anastasia announced. "And I am not going in until my own room is ready. Do you hear me? I am not!"

"As you wish," her mother finally said. "I agree with Amelie, but by all means stay outside, if that is what you want. I only hope you and your pride don't catch cold together."

"I know what you are doing!" Anastasia cried out, her voice as petulant as a child's. "You're trying to scare me. It isn't going to work. I will not sit in a kitchen like some common girl."

"I don't see why not," her mother observed, her own voice cool and careful. "When you have no problem behaving like one. Still, you have made your choice, and you may now abide by it. I will send Cendrillon to fetch you when your room is ready." She turned to Old Mathilde. "If you will be so good as to show those of us who wish to go in the way?"

"You cannot make me!" Anastasia cried, stamping one booted foot upon the cobblestones. "You can't! Haven't we all been made to do enough?"

What her mother might have answered then, I cannot say, for Anastasia stamped her other foot as well. And at that, as if startled from dreams of a clean, dry stall and a pile of fresh hay, the closest of the carriage horses suddenly screamed and reared straight up. Its great front forelegs pawed the air. Within an instant, the second horse had reared as well. The carriage jerked backward as the coachman struggled with the reins. Niccolo spun around.

And then, suddenly, Raoul was there. Just as Niccolo reached for Amelie, pulling her away from the horse, shielding her with his own body, Raoul caught Anastasia up into his arms. Lifting her, then whirling her away from the horse's hooves just as they came slashing down. The coachman gave the horses their heads, sending them flying around the courtyard, then back out onto the road. The dappled gray Niccolo had ridden snorted and pranced, but, at a sharp command from Raoul, it grew still and quiet once more.

"Your coachman is a wise man, lady," Raoul said, into the great silence that suddenly filled the courtyard. "He will let them run off their fear. It won't take long, not on these muddy roads."

Only then did he look down at the young woman he held

in his arms. "They will be back by the time your room is prepared, my fine young mistress. Though, if you were my daughter, such foolish behavior would earn you a night in the barn."

For a moment, Anastasia stared up at him through wide and startled eyes. Then the color in her face flamed bright red.

"Put. Me. Down," she said through clenched teeth, spacing each word out slowly and carefully, as if Raoul might be too simple to understand them otherwise.

"Do you hear me? Put me down right now! I did not give you permission to touch me. You're nothing but a stable boy and you reek of horses. Now I shall need a bath as well, to get rid of the smell."

Raoul let one of his arms drop away so suddenly Anastasia gave a startled cry as her legs swung down. With a bone-jarring smack, her feet connected with the cobblestones. But I noticed that he kept his second arm around her back until he was certain she was steady on her feet.

"In that case, you will have to reconsider your plan to avoid the kitchen," he said. "For that is where we heat the water for our baths at the end of the world."

He moved toward the gray, even as my stepmother began to hurry toward her daughters. "I will see to the horse," he said to Niccolo. "For something tells me you may be needed elsewhere."

Entirely without warning, he gave a wolfish grin, and Niccolo grinned back.

"Welcome home, Niccolo," he added.

"My girls," Chantal de Saint-Andre said, as she held out her arms. "Are you both unharmed?"

"I am fine, Mother," Amelie replied. She did not move immediately to her mother's arms, I noticed, but stood her ground. "For which I must thank you, Niccolo."

She extended her hand. Niccolo took it, holding it by no more than the fingertips, and executed what I could only assume was a perfect court bow.

"It is my pleasure to serve you, Lady Amelie," he said as he slowly let her fingers go. "Though I hope you will not be insulted if I say I hope we never have to do that again."

"And I hope *you* will not be insulted when I say that I agree," Amelie answered with a smile.

"Well, I am far from fine," Anastasia remarked tartly, but I saw the way she went into her mother's arms and clung. "I am cold and tired, and now I smell like horses besides."

Chantal de Saint-Andre rested her chin atop her daughter's head. Just for a moment, she closed her eyes.

"I think," she said, as she opened them again, "that it is time for us all to go inside. And if you even think of arguing with me, my lovely Anastasia, you will smell like many more things than horses, for I will take that young man's advice and send you to sleep in the barn."

"You wouldn't!" Anastasia exclaimed.

"Oh, yes, I would," said her mother. "This long, cold day has gone on long enough. Let us see if a kitchen fire cannot begin to set us all to rights."

And so, with Old Mathilde leading the way, the mother and sisters I had wished for walked up the steps and into the great stone house.

Seven

"HOW MUCH LONGER ARE YOU GOING TO WAIT BEFORE YOU tell them?"

I gave a pillowcase a smart snap, then pinned it to the clothesline. Several weeks had gone by and we had reached the end of March. I was taking advantage of a rare sunny day to do an extra washing. With three new people, all of them fine ladies, the last few weeks had brought a number of changes to the great stone house.

The day after Chantal de Saint-Andre's arrival, and with her blessing, Old Mathilde had gone to the village at the foot of our cliff and hired extra help. Susanne and Charlotte now had more hands in the kitchen. Joseph and Robert, help with the grounds. Old Mathilde had two new girls to help handle the housework. Though we had never neglected it, in less than a month, the great stone house had once again begun to shine with life. I wondered if my father realized what he had done.

With so many other people to look after the house, caring for my stepmother and stepsisters had fallen to me. In the weeks since their arrival, I had acquired several new skills: I now knew how to dress a lady's hair, the best way to remove wrinkles from silk, how to starch and iron a fine linen collar. Chantal and Amelie had been calm and patient in their instructions. Anastasia had been a tyrant.

It was her sheets I was hanging on the line. Though they had been freshly changed just this morning, she had refused, point blank, to sleep upon them, insisting they smelled as damp and musty as the weather we had endured all month. My personal opinion was that she simply liked the fact that she could order me about. Giving other people orders made Anastasia feel important.

"And just when would you suggest I tell them?" I inquired of Raoul now. "Before or after I pin up their hair and fasten their gowns? Here, help me with this."

I tossed the end of one of Anastasia's sheets in Raoul's direction. Together, we pulled it along the length of the clothesline, then pegged it so it wouldn't blow away. Except for when he came to the kitchen for his meals, Raoul spent most of his time in the stable, or out of doors. His mood had been as glowering as the dark March weather, particularly once Niccolo had gone back to court after he made sure my stepmother and stepsisters were safely settled.

"How should I know when you should tell them?" Raoul asked now, his tone grumpy. "The way she treats you is wrong. I know that much." I didn't have to ask who *she* was. We both knew well enough.

"I don't particularly care for it myself," I answered, as we began to peg the second sheet onto the line. "But I can hardly just blurt out who I am at this point. I have to find a way to do it that doesn't make it seem as if I've played them false. If I simply announce who I am now, it's going to look as if we've all deliberately made fools of them."

"All right. I guess I can see that," Raoul said grudgingly. "What does Old Mathilde say?"

"Nothing."

Raoul paused, a clothespin in midair. "What do you mean, nothing?"

"I mean nothing," I answered, my voice grumpy now. "She hasn't mentioned it at all. Not even once."

Raoul made a face. "That doesn't sound like her."

"No," I said. "It doesn't. Which leads me to believe there's a lesson lurking just around the corner. I really am thinking about the situation, Raoul. Sometimes, it feels like all I think about. I didn't just wish for any old stepmother and stepsisters. I wished for some that I might love, some who might love me. But they can't do that if they don't know who I am, and they can't know who I am unless I tell them. The whole situation makes my head hurt, if you want to know the truth."

"Do you love me?" Raoul asked suddenly.

"Of course I do," I said. "What does that have to do with anything?"

"You don't know who I am. None of us do," Raoul answered quietly.

"That's not true," I replied, somewhat hotly. "You are Raoul. You're generous and grumpy, the best horseman in the county. You like peach pie better than apple, and Old Mathilde's ginger cookies best of all. I would trust you with my life. I may not know where you came from, but that's not the same as not knowing who you are."

"Some days, it feels that way to me," Raoul said. "And I like cherry pie best of all."

"Did I leave out deliberately contrary?" I said sweetly. "Incredibly annoying?"

"I don't really smell of horse, do I?"

I opened my mouth, then closed it again, as I felt my hand ball into a fist at my side. *Anastasia again,* I thought. *That foolish girl has a great deal to answer for.* It took a lot to get under Raoul's skin. She had done it the very first night, and now her cruel and thoughtless words were a part of him.

"The question isn't whether or not you smell of horses,"

I answered. "But whether or not horses smell. Specifically, whether or not they smell bad."

"Anastasia seems to think so," Raoul said. "She made that clear enough."

"Why do you care what she thinks?" I asked. "She may be as old as we are, but she's nothing more than a spoiled child. The way she treated you is just as bad as the way she treats me, Raoul. And if she thinks you smell bad after working with the horses, I suggest you pay her a visit after you've been mucking out the pigsty."

Raoul's lips gave a reluctant twitch. "You're trying to tell me I'm being an idiot," he said.

"No," I replied. "I'm trying to tell you Anastasia is one. The fact that she hurt your feelings doesn't make her right, you know."

"I do know that," Raoul said. "It's just—"

"It's just that even idiots sometimes have a way with words," I said. "And some words have sharp tongues. I know."

"I *am* being an idiot," Raoul said.

"Well, if you insist," I replied. I picked up the empty laundry basket, settled it onto one hip. "I should go back inside. Just this morning, Anastasia suddenly discovered half a dozen dresses in immediate need of mending. She'll pitch a fit if I don't at least get started on them."

Before I quite realized what he intended, Raoul leaned forward and kissed me on the cheek. I felt my face flame, put my hand to the spot, as if to hold the kiss in place.

"What was that for?"

"To thank you," Raoul replied, his own cheeks ruddy now. Displays of affection were rare between us, between Raoul and anyone. "You're a good friend to have, Rilla."

"As are you," I said. "And I'm going to remind you of those fine words the next time I annoy you."

A light I knew very well came into Raoul's eyes. "Maybe you should just start now."

I laughed suddenly, threw my arms around his neck, and kissed him back. "I'll see you at supper," I said. "Don't forget to wash up."

"Oh, I intend to," Raoul said. "But first, I think I'll just go and see how the pigs are doing."

He was whistling as he turned on his heel and sauntered across the courtyard.

"Oh, Cendrillon," Anastasia said as I entered her room in obedience to the bright *come in* that had answered my knock. "There you are. I was beginning to think this dreadful March wind had blown you out to sea, you were taking so long."

She was standing at the window, staring out toward the water, wearing a white dress with pale pink flowers embroidered all over it. It was the perfect foil for her dark beauty. All of a sudden, I felt a strange lump in my throat. Would I be beautiful, too, if I had a dress like this? If I had dozens of them? What might I look like, if I could dress like the nobleman's daughter that I was?

In the next second, I grew ashamed of myself. *Perhaps you shouldn't be so quick to think you know yourself or anyone else, Cendrillon,* I thought. Jealousy had never been a part of my nature, not until Anastasia had arrived.

She turned from the window. "I am waiting," she said, in a tone like cold, clear glass. I could almost feel the way it pressed against me, trying to find a way to cut.

I hesitated, sensing the trap, but unable to see how I could avoid stepping into it anyhow. I gave up the struggle and spoke.

"For what?"

"Not even you can possibly be so stupid," Anastasia snapped. "For my apology, of course."

"Your apology!" I exclaimed before I could help myself. Abruptly, I could feel my own temper start to rise. I was spending hours agonizing over how to tell Anastasia, her mother, and her sister the truth about who I was in a way that wouldn't hurt their feelings, and this vain and silly girl stood there in her finery demanding an apology for only she knew what.

"Why on earth should I apologize to you? I haven't done anything wrong."

"That is a matter of opinion," Anastasia huffed. "As servants do not have opinions, none that count anyway, the only opinion in this room is mine. And I say you owe me an apology for keeping me waiting. You are here to serve me, not to chat in the yard with foul-smelling stable boys."

"Raoul is not foul-smelling," I said hotly.

"Don't be absurd," Anastasia replied. She gave a sniff, as if to emphasize her words. "I can practically smell the stables from here. Girls like you can be dismissed for your kind of behavior, you know."

Abruptly, I felt my temper reach its boiling point.

"I *am* sorry," I said sweetly, and caught the satisfaction that flashed across Anastasia's face. "But then I'm just a plain country girl, unaccustomed to the ways of fine ladies. Explain to me how hanging out sheets that didn't need washing in the first place is cause to have me dismissed."

Two bright spots of color flared in my stepsister's cheeks. "How dare you?" she cried. "How dare you speak to me in such a way? I can have you dismissed for anything, anytime I want to. And don't think I didn't see the way you touched each other, because I did. I saw it all."

"Then you are blind as well as ill-tempered and spoiled. Raoul and I have known each other since we were two weeks old. He put spiders in my hair, and I put garter snakes in both his boots. We are hardly likely to be flirting over a clothesline."

"If you think for one moment that I care what the two of you do together—" Anastasia began.

"I don't," I said, ruthlessly cutting her off. "The simple truth is, Raoul and I both try not to think about you at all."

A terrible silence filled the room. Anastasia's cheeks were pale as milk now. And I saw, to my absolute horror, that her eyes were filled with tears.

"Oh, Cendrillon," Amelie's voice slipped quietly into the room. "How fortunate. I was hoping you might help me with something, and here you are."

Anastasia turned away, moved to the window seat, and sat down upon it with such force that the cushions beneath her sighed. *Oh, Cendrillon,* I thought to myself. *What have you just done?*

"Of course I will help you," I said, as I turned to Amelie. "If you will just give me a moment to collect your sister's mending."

"Actually," Anastasia said in a brittle voice. "I find that I have changed my mind. Instead of mending just these few dresses, I think it will be necessary to attend to my entire wardrobe."

She turned away from the window to face me again, and, though her eyes were still too bright, I could see that they were dry. I felt my stomach give a funny little twist.

"I'm not going to be stuck out here in the country forever, you know," Anastasia went on. "And neither is Amelie. Etienne de Brabant is an important man at court, and daughters of marriageable age are an asset, whether he wants them or not. I intend to be ready when he sends for us." She tilted her head, and her eyes as they met mine were cold as snow. In them, I read dislike and a challenge.

"You understand what I require?"

"I do," I acknowledged. And it was nothing less than looking over every single item in her entire wardrobe. Every seam of every dress. Every stitch which fastened on a ribbon or a seed pearl. Every hem and button. Everything must be in perfect order. I had no doubt it was a task she could make stretch on for weeks.

"I am pleased to hear it," Anastasia replied in a sweet voice. "Naturally, I will need to supervise you closely, to make certain the job is done right." She tilted her head in the other direction. "A pity you will have no more time to flirt with stable boys."

She turned her back on me then, her gesture a clear sign of dismissal.

"Please help my sister with whatever she needs, then do me the pleasure of staying out of my sight for the rest of the day," she went on. "I'm sure you and I will both appreciate having one less thing to think about."

"As you wish," I said. And, to my surprise, Anastasia's head whipped back around.

"It shall be as I wish," she said fiercely, and now her eyes were hot and bright. "Do you hear me? I say it shall. Now get out of my room. I'm tired of looking at you. I'm tired of every single thing about this dreadful place."

She turned back to the window. For a moment, I thought that Amelie would go to her. Instead, she gave a little sigh.

"Come with me, Cendrillon, if you please," she said. She preceded me into the hall. I closed the door quietly behind us, then hurried to keep up as Amelie had already set off at a brisk pace down the corridor.

"I think this place is beautiful," she said after a moment. "Especially the house. I didn't think I would. I didn't think I'd like anything about this place when we first arrived."

"What made you change your mind?" I asked, then cursed myself for an idiot when Amelie stopped abruptly and turned around. I had spoken to her like an equal, as if I had the right to ask her what she felt and thought. As far as she was concerned, of course, I did not. I was no more than a servant in Amelie's eyes. The fact that she treated me better than her sister did didn't change things a bit.

"You have lived here a long time, I think," Amelie observed. "And you love this place."

"I have lived here all my life," I answered, deciding to focus on the first statement and let the second go. "I was born here, in fact. Old Mathilde delivered me."

Amelie's expression brightened. There was something about her that always reminded me of a sparrow, though she was neither drab nor plump. But she had a sparrow's bright eyes. A bird's darting interest and intelligence.

"I did not know that," she said. She turned back around. If we had truly been equals, she might have inquired about the rest of my family, my mother and father, but she did not. Instead, she set off once more along the hall, her pace so brisk I had to almost trot along behind her to keep up.

"But it makes you the perfect person to answer my question," she went on.

"What question is that?" I asked, as Amelie finally came to a halt.

"I am hoping you can tell me," she said, "why this door is kept locked. None of the others are. I know. I've checked them myself."

I swallowed past a suddenly dry throat. I had been so busy worrying about giving myself away, I had failed to notice that Amelie was heading straight toward my mother's door. *Tell her. Tell her all of it, the truth about who you are,* I thought. There might never be a better time.

I opened my mouth, but the words I wished to say seemed to stick inside my throat. If I claimed Constanze d'Este as my mother, then I must also claim Etienne de Brabant as my father. Etienne de Brabant, who had sent his new wife and step-daughters to the great stone house without bothering to inform them of my existence, so great was his desire to deny I was even alive.

How would Amelie take the news if I told her? Would she be kind? Would she even believe me at all? But it was think-ing of what Anastasia's reaction might be that finally made up my mind. Her scorn I could bear, but not her pity, and, in that moment, pity seemed the only possible outcome of the telling of a tale such as mine.

"This room belonged to Etienne de Brabant's first wife," I finally answered, deciding there was no point in telling a lie. All Amelie would have to do would be to ask someone else. "He locked the door and threw away the key when she died."

Amelie put her hands on her hips, pursing her lips and putting her head to one side. She studied the locked door as if it were a puzzle, just waiting to be solved.

"And has it never been opened since? Has no one even tried?"

"Never," I said. And it occurred to me suddenly that not even I had ever been through that door, not since I had gone out it on the day that I was born. I had no idea what my mother's room contained.

"What was her name, do you know?"

"Her name was Constanze d'Este," I said.

"Ah," Amelie answered, and her voice was like a sigh. She took her hands from her hips and, to my surprise, laid one palm very gently on the surface of my mother's door.

"I have heard of Constanze d'Este," Amelie went on softly. "Whispers of her name were everywhere when we were at court, particularly on the day my mother and Etienne de Brabant spoke their wedding vows. Constanze d'Este's beauty had no equal, I heard them say, and the loss of her tore a great hole in Etienne de Brabant's heart. One that has never been filled, and never will be."

She turned her head to look at me. "Does that mean his heart is empty, do you suppose?"

"I honestly don't know," I said.

Amelie let her hand drop. "Nor do I. And neither, I think, does Maman, not that it will make much difference, in either the long or the short run. There is no chance of love between them. Maman's heart is not whole, either. The king has seen to that by breaking his promise."

"I don't understand," I said. "I'm sorry."

Amelie stood for a moment, gazing at the locked door. She seemed to have completely forgotten the fact that I was a servant, so great was her need to confide in someone.

"My mother and the king grew up together," she said. "Both made marriages of state, though I think my parents' marriage was happier than the king's ever was. When my father was killed in a border war, the king made my mother a promise that, if she married again, it could be for love."

"Then why did he marry her to Etienne de Brabant?" I asked.

Amelie sighed. "That is a very good question," she said. "I think it is because he is the leader of the queen's faction at court. With the queen's brother on a throne of his own now, who can say what brother and sister might plot? But if Etienne de Brabant were married to someone loyal to the king, someone he trusts . . ."

She broke off and shook her head. "But my new stepfather is clever. As soon as the marriage festivities were over, he packed us up and sent us off. My mother can hardly keep an eye on him from this great distance."

"So the king has accomplished nothing," I said softly. "Save betraying your mother's trust."

"That's it exactly," Amelie replied. "She's stuck in a loveless marriage, and we're all stuck here, so very far from home."

"Spring is coming almost any day now," I said. It seemed paltry consolation, but surely it was better than none. "Things will get better then. I promise."

My stepsister gave me a trembling smile. "Thank you, Cendrillon," she said. "You are really very kind. But for obvious reasons, I think I would prefer it if we avoided making promises, at least for the time being."

Before I could answer, she drew in a deep breath, and stepped back from the door. "But what am I saying?" she said, as she turned away. "Of course things will be better when the spring truly comes. Spring works wonders everywhere, don't you think? And naturally you will not mention the conversation we have had today to anyone."

I opened my mouth to give an assurance, but Amelie had already set off down the hall. *I am back to being a servant,* I thought. At the landing at the head of the stairs, Amelie halted abruptly.

"Where is Constanze d'Este buried? Do you know?"

"In her garden," I answered. "On the far side of the house. I can take you there, if you like."

"I believe I would like that," Amelie said slowly. "But not today. Today I have discovered quite enough."

"In April, when the daffodils bloom," I suddenly blurted out.

Amelie's eyebrows rose. "That sounds lovely, thank you, Cendrillon. I am fond of daffodils. There are great fields of them where I grew up."

"Where is your home?"

A strange expression flashed into Amelie's eyes. There and gone so quickly I didn't quite have time to figure out what it was.

"This is my home, now, Cendrillon," she said.

Then she turned and was gone.

SPRING CAME IN A GREAT AND COLORFUL RUSH. IN APRIL THE daffodils bloomed. In May, the peonies. In June, the roses. The fruit trees in the orchard gave every sign that this would be a year when they would behave themselves and provide the kind of fruit they were supposed to.

As the weather grew warmer, both Amelie and Anastasia began to spend more time out of doors, often in my mother's garden. Amelie in particular seemed drawn to it, even beginning to go so far as to work in the garden herself. Since the day I had taken her to see Constanze d'Este's grave, the same day I finally finished the seemingly endless task of going through Anastasia's dresses, as it happened, it seemed to me that Amelie was working hard to make her peace with the circumstances that had brought her to the great stone house.

Even Anastasia seemed calmer now that the weather had improved. She would sit on a stone bench in the shade, her own sun hat firmly in place upon her head, chiding Amelie for the fact that hers had fallen off and that her hands and nails were filthy from working the soil. To which Amelie always replied that some young men found freckles attractive, and dirt could be washed off. But it was a gentle sort of teasing, as if the warmth of the weather had mellowed them both. Now that she was finished torturing me with the endless examination of her wardrobe, Anastasia seemed content to leave me alone. Neither of us mentioned Raoul again.

The only one who did not seem warmed by the change in the weather was my stepmother. She roamed the house and grounds like a phantom as if unable to settle, to find peace anywhere, her skin still as fine and pale as the winter's day upon which she had first crossed our threshold. More and more often, I was reminded of my first impression of her: that she was like a spring in full flood with its surface still encased in ice.

At first, I had believed that this was a sign of the strength of her own will, her refusal to give way to the turmoil and despair which filled her mind and heart. But as the days and weeks went by, I began to wonder whether or not Chantal de Saint-Andre had made herself a prisoner to what she felt.

If my father's heart was empty, then my stepmother's was too full. And I wondered what would happen when the ice finally broke.

"Poor lady," Susanne sighed while preparing dinner one night. She was chopping vigorously, the knife thunking against the cutting board. Susanne had made getting my stepmother to eat her own personal crusade. To that end, she tried a different dish each night. Tonight's attempt involved chicken and vegetables cooked on top of the stove. The smell of it filled the whole house.

"Forced into a loveless marriage, then packed off like a piece of furniture that's gone out of style. She'll waste away to nothing, you mark my words, and then Etienne de Brabant will have what he wants."

"What do you mean?" I asked from the far end of the table, where I was preparing a great pile of green beans. I had kept the conversation I had shared with Amelie outside my mother's door strictly to myself. But there wasn't one person in all the great stone house who believed my father had married Chantal de Saint-Andre for love.

"What does he want?" I asked now.

"Why, to be rid of her, of course," Susanne snorted. "Why else would he send her to the ends of the earth and then leave her alone, without any kind of word, for five whole months? It would eat me alive with frustration and fury, I promise you that. If you ask me, unless something happens to change the way things are going, that man will be a widower before the year is out."

"Then it's fortunate nobody did ask," Old Mathilde's voice suddenly sliced through the room, sharper than any kitchen knife. Susanne dropped hers with a clatter and pressed a hand to her heart.

"Gracious, Mathilde," she exclaimed. "Don't you know better than to startle a body like that?"

"I know better than to indulge in idle gossip," Old Mathilde replied, and I saw the way she glanced at me out of the corner of my eye. "You may hold whatever opinions you like, Susanne, but in the future, I would appreciate it if you kept them to yourself. This house is troubled enough without your wild surmises.

"Our mistress would like a cup of tea," she went on in a more quiet voice. "Cendrillon, perhaps you would be so good as to make one and to take it to her."

"Of course I will," I said, as I finished the last of the beans, gathered them up, and dumped them into their cooking pot. I set it on the back of the stove and put the tea kettle on to boil. Susanne was chopping once again, the sound of the knife informing all who heard it and knew how to listen that her nose was out of joint.

"Susanne didn't mean anything, Mathilde," I felt obliged to say. "Nothing bad, anyhow. And she's right, you know. Chantal de Saint-Andre does not look well. Do you think she has an illness?"

Old Mathilde shook her head. "Not one that comes from any outside cause. As for the inside one, well . . ." Her voice trailed off.

Steam began to rush from the spout of the kettle. I took it from the hob, poured a little water into the teapot to warm it. Then I emptied it out, added the tea, and poured the boiling water over all. I set it on a tray, then wrapped the pot in red flannel to help keep it warm. Once upon a time, I had been kept warm in much the same manner. The thought brought a sudden smile.

"Didn't you make seed cake this morning?" I asked Old Mathilde. She gave a nod. "Chantal likes that, doesn't she? Perhaps I'll take some of that along as well."

"That is very thoughtful of you," Old Mathilde said, as I found the loaf of cake and began to slice it. "She is in the sun room."

The sun room was small and filled with light, even in winter. Tucked into a far corner of the main floor of the house, it had windows on two sides. One looked straight out over the ocean, the other, toward the tops of the trees in the orchards. Chantal often spent time there. It was her favorite room in the house.

I cut two thick slices of seed cake and put them on my favorite plate, one with sunflowers painted on it. I fetched the cup and saucer to match, placed both upon the tray beside the teapot. Sugar in its bowl came next; milk in a sturdy little jug. I added a blue napkin, then hefted the tray.

"That's nicely done and no mistake," Susanne said, her tone approving. "Lovely looking tray like that would cheer anybody up. Look sharp she doesn't eat too much and spoil her dinner, mind you."

"I will, Susanne," I promised.

I carried the tray upstairs, careful to hold it level, then made my way to the sun room. Chantal de Saint-Andre was sitting in a chair, a shawl around her shoulders, her legs tucked under her like a child. One of her elbows rested on the arm of the chair. She had her chin on one hand, and her eyes gazed straight out at nothing.

"I've brought your tea, ma'am," I said from the open doorway.

My stepmother turned toward me then. "Oh," she said. "It is you, Cendrillon. I was expecting Old Mathilde."

I hesitated, uncertain whether I should go back or forward. "I could fetch her, if you like."

Chantal de Saint-Andre seemed to give herself a little mental shake. "No," she said. "Of course not. You brought the tea, you said? Thank you. Tea will be most welcome. I know that it is spring, but I cannot seem to get warm."

I moved forward then, placing the tray on a low table near the chair. "I brought some of Old Mathilde's seed cake," I went on, as I began the ritual of pouring out. "But I fear we are both under strict instructions from Susanne. I am to make certain you don't eat too much cake and spoil your appetite for supper."

At this, my stepmother actually smiled. "I seem to recall giving my daughters similar instructions, once upon a time. Tell Susanne that I will be a good girl."

I lifted the cup and saucer and extended it toward her. Halfway in the act of reaching for it, Chantal de Saint-Andre's hand paused in midair.

"Oh," she said. "Sunflowers."

Not until then did I realize what I had done. I had prepared the tray for my stepmother precisely as I would have for myself. Choosing not the fanciest plate or cup and saucer, but the ones that made me feel cheerful, even on the gloomiest of days. I felt the way my hand wished to tremble, but held it steady.

"If you do not care for them," I said. "I can bring you something else."

"Sunflowers are my favorite flower in all the world," my stepmother said, almost as if she were speaking to herself. "In the summer, there are great fields of them along the roadsides on the lands where I raised my daughters, and where I, myself, grew up. The old folks say they have never been planted, but every year, there they are. I have seen many growing things since we came here, but not a single sunflower. I think it is too cold for them to grow."

As if to prove her point, she shivered, and drew her shawl a little more tightly around her shoulders.

"Where is it?" I asked, hardly daring to breathe. "The place where you grew up?"

"In the very center of the country," my stepmother replied. "They say our very first king was born there, and so it is our country's heart. The land is flat, the fields are fertile, and the sun is warm."

For a moment, I thought she would say more. Instead she leaned forward, took the saucer between her thumb and forefinger. I let go.

"Did you prepare this tray yourself?" she asked.

"Yes, ma'am," I answered.

"Then I thank you, Cendrillon." She took a sip of tea, closing her eyes as she swallowed, as if the simple action gave her just a taste of the peace she so desperately sought. She opened her eyes, then set the cup and saucer on the wide arm of the chair.

"Was there something else?"

"It can be beautiful here, too," I heard myself blurt out. "You just have to know how to look, and . . ." My voice faltered but I forced it to go on. "I wish you could be happy here. All of you. I'm sorry that you're not."

My stepmother jerked, as if I'd poked her with a pin. I bit down, hard, on the tip of my tongue, my eyes suddenly fascinated by the hardwood floor. *Fool, idiot,* I thought. *She thinks you're a serving girl. What difference could it possibly make to you whether she and her daughters are happy here or not?*

"Look at me, please, Cendrillon," Chantal de Saint-Andre said in a firm, soft voice. I lifted my eyes. For several absolutely silent seconds, my stepmother and I gazed at each other. I watched her cheeks flush, then go absolutely bloodless.

"You pity me," she said. And in that moment, I realized that she had seen her own face, reflected in my eyes.

Before I could answer, she made a quick movement, as if to push what she had seen away. Her hand struck the saucer on the arm of the chair, sending it and the cup flying. Hot liquid arced through the air, then splashed to the floor. The cup and saucer hit the hardwood and were dashed to pieces. My stepmother gave a heartbroken cry.

Even as I knelt to pick up the shards, I heard the sound of fast moving feet. Amelie and Anastasia burst into the sun room, one right after the other. But it was Anastasia who spoke first.

"You dreadful girl," she cried, as she moved quickly to her mother. "What have you done?"

"Nothing," I gasped out. "That is, I didn't mean . . ."

To call you here in the first place, I thought. Not at such a terrible cost.

I had made a wish and it had been answered. Didn't that make their misery all my fault? I felt a sudden sharp pain as one of the broken pieces of the saucer cut into my hand.

"How dare you?" Anastasia demanded. "How dare you lie? Look at her. You've made her cry, and she never does that. Not even on the day the king made her marry the queen's man. My mother is not a coward. She is brave and strong. You must have done something truly terrible to make her do this, and I want to know what it is right now."

"Oh, stop it, Anastasia," Amelie said. "Can't you see she's cut herself?"

"I don't care if she bleeds to death," Anastasia all but shouted.

"No one is going to bleed to death," Chantal de Saint-Andre said in a calm and terrible voice. With the backs of her hands, she wiped the tears from her pale cheeks with quick, angry gestures, as if as furious with herself as Anastasia was with me. "Please stop shouting, Anastasia. My head hurts enough as it is."

Anastasia took a stumbling step back, as if her mother's words had made her lose her balance.

"You are defending her," she whispered. "That horrible girl made you cry and now you are taking her side."

"Cendrillon is not a horrible girl," her mother answered, as she got up from the chair. "And there is no question of taking sides. I broke a cup and saucer, and that's all there is to that."

Before I realized what she intended, she knelt beside me. "Let me see your hand, Cendrillon."

"It's nothing," I protested, though I knew the cut was deep, a great slash across one palm. Blood flowed over its surface to trickle through my fingers. "If you will just let me go for Old Mathilde."

"I'll go," Amelie offered now. She picked up the tray.

"What are you doing?" Anastasia shrieked. "Put that down."

"Be quiet, Anastasia," Amelie said briskly. She walked quickly from the room, her shoes making sharp sounds against the hardwood floor.

"I'm sorry," I whispered, as I gazed at my hand, cradled between my stepmother's. "I didn't mean for any of this to happen. I'm so sorry."

"I think that's enough apologies for one afternoon," Chantal said, her tone the brisk match of Amelie's. "It is only a cup and saucer."

Oh, no. It is much, much more than that, I thought. And if she knew how much, one thing seemed certain: This woman I had wished for could never learn to love me.

"There is still the plate," I said.

Chantal sat back, still cradling my hand in hers. "I believe you are growing light-headed," she said. "What are you talking about?"

"The plate," I said once more. "With the seed cake on it. It has sunflowers, too. Not everything is broken."

"I see," my stepmother said, and for the second time that day, she looked into my eyes. This time, I was the one who saw my own reflection: an image of a girl just on the cusp of womanhood.

A girl with tears and secrets in her eyes.

Nine

THERE WERE NO MORE CHORES FOR ME THE REST OF THAT DAY,
nor for several more besides. The cut was both long and deep;
my hand was stiff and sore. At Old Mathilde's insistence, I slept
on a cot in a corner of the kitchen, much as I had done when
I was a child. She could keep a better eye on me that way, she
said, without having to climb up and down all the stairs to my
room at the very top of the house. Too many stairs were hard
on old bones, or so she claimed.

The days slid into August, and the weather stayed hot and
fine. Still the ice inside my stepmother did not quite thaw.
Anastasia stopped speaking to me altogether, not even to give me
orders. The day she discovered that Amelie had traded a fancy

dress to one of the village girls so that she might have a simple one to tramp around outside in, she all but stopped speaking to Amelie as well. In her new dress, which she felt free to get as dirty as she liked, a sturdy pair of boots, and her sun hat, Amelie took to prowling the grounds. She was always popping up in unexpected places, poking into long-forgotten corners both inside and out. There were times, and many of them, too, when it seemed to me that she was searching for something.

Slowly, the wound on my hand healed. But I could not quite forget the wound I had seen in my stepmother's eyes. A wound I greatly feared I had helped to inflict myself.

"I just keep thinking it's all my fault," I said one day to Old Mathilde. It was midmorning, the heat of the day not yet upon us. Old Mathilde was standing at the stove stirring a great kettle of blackberry jam. My hand back to normal now, I was shucking ears of corn.

"If I hadn't wished for them, they wouldn't have come. And if they hadn't come, they wouldn't all be so unhappy."

"Tut, now," Old Mathilde said, as she added sugar to the pot. "Nothing is ever quite as simple as that and you should know it. You sound like your father when you speak so."

I yanked at a corn husk. It gave way with a shrieking sound. "There's no need to insult me," I said. "I'm just trying to figure out what to do to make things right."

Old Mathilde's spoon circled in the pot like a hawk after a mouse. "What makes you think that responsibility lies with you alone?" she asked. "You made a wish, that much is true, but you did not wish for anyone to be made unhappy. You made a wish for love. In my experience, such wishes have a way of coming true in the end, which is not the same as saying the journey isn't difficult and long."

I sat for a moment, pondering her words. The noise of Old Mathilde's spoon, swishing against the bottom of the cast-iron pot, was the only sound.

"Have I ever told you the story of how your parents met?" she inquired at last. If she had asked me if I realized I had suddenly grown two heads, I could not have been more surprised.

"Never," I said. "And you know that perfectly well."

"No one ever dreamed that they would love each other," Old Mathilde went on, as if I hadn't spoken at all. "Least of all Etienne and Constanze themselves. Their marriage was arranged to help secure an alliance, of course. But I think it's fair to say that your father loved your mother from the first moment that he saw her, and that for her to love him took no longer."

"Love at first sight," I said, my voice hushed, the ears of corn I should have been shucking entirely forgotten. "It really happens, then?"

"On occasion." Old Mathilde nodded. "I've heard it runs in families, if you must know. Your mother's love was much like her garden. Its roots went deep, though it wasn't always showy. But your father's love was like a diamond, hard and bright, so dazzling it hurt the eyes to look upon it. His love for your mother, hers for him, were the greatest astonishments, the greatest treasures, of his life."

"And I took them away," I said, as I felt a swift, hot pain spear straight through my heart.

"That is certainly what Etienne believes, or what he says he does," Old Mathilde answered. "Help me with this now."

She lifted the pot from the heat, and, together, we worked to ladle the steaming liquid into jars. Carefully, Old Mathilde spooned hot wax atop each one to seal the jam in, then set them in a neat row on the pantry shelf. They glowed like purple jewels.

"They are beautiful," I said. "Can we have pancakes for break-fast tomorrow morning?"

"I believe we might do that," Old Mathilde answered as she put an arm around my shoulders.

"I'll do the washing up," I said, as I leaned against her. "You should go sit down. You've been standing up most of the morning."

"I believe we might do that, too," Old Mathilde said with a smile. She sat down in the chair I had vacated. I filled a pitcher of water from the kitchen pump, then poured it into the jam kettle.

"Wait a few minutes," Mathilde instructed. "Let the water do its work while the pot cools down. Come and sit beside me for a moment. There is something more I wish to say."

I dried my hands on my apron and sat down across the table

from her. Old Mathilde reached across and took my hands in hers.

"Your mother loved your father, Cendrillon. To the end of her last breath, with all her heart. And she loved you just as much as she loved him. That kind of love does not simply pack its bags and depart, even when the heart that brought it into being ceases to beat. Love so joyfully and freely given can never be taken away. It is never truly gone."

"Then where is it?" I whispered. "Why does it seem so hard to find?"

"It is all around you," Old Mathilde said. "It lives in every beat of your own heart. This is what your mother knew your father would never understand, for she saw him truly, and she foresaw that his grief would dazzle just as his love did. It would blind him.

"To heal, we must do more than grieve. We must also find a way to mourn."

"I'm not so sure I understand the difference," I said.

Old Mathilde gave my hands a squeeze. "I am not surprised, for the difference is a fine one. But when you figure it out, you will know what to do about many things, I think.

"Remember that yours is not the only heart that may be wishing for love."

Late that night, I could not sleep. I might have convinced myself it was because my bedroom was too hot, for my room was right beneath the roof and the day had been warm. I might have convinced myself it was the light of the full moon, shining through my window, that was making me toss and turn so often.

I might have convinced myself of many things, if I had been willing to lie.

But because I was not, I threw back my rumpled sheet and got out of bed. I made my silent way down to the kitchen, slipped my shawl from its peg, and tucked my feet into my wooden garden clogs. I took the long, thin knife Susanne used for boning chickens from its slot in the wooden block and wrapped the blade in a towel. Then I let myself out the kitchen door, heading in the direction of the pumpkin patch. I had no need to take a lantern, for the face of the moon shone like a beacon in the clear night sky.

Though they were far from ripe, anyone with eyes could see that, unlike last year's wide variety, this year, each and every vine in the pumpkin patch was busy producing pumpkins of precisely the same kind. Ones just like those I had planted on my mother's grave, in spite of the fact that I had saved no seeds from them. They glowed a deep and mysterious green in the moonlight.

I took a deep breath, then knelt down among them. Before I would be able to sleep, there was something I must discover, a task I must perform.

Sliding the knife from the towel, I sliced neatly through

the stem of the pumpkin at my feet and set it upright in front of me. Then, without stopping to think and so lose my nerve, I plunged the knife through the pumpkin's skin and into the flesh beneath, slicing first through one side, and then the other. Setting the knife on the ground at my feet, I wiggled my fingers into the gap I had made in the top, then pried the pumpkin open. The two halves parted with a high, tearing sound. The pungent smell of pumpkin rose up sharply.

Not rotten inside, I thought. *Not rotten at all, but firm and pure and sound.* And in that moment, I had the answer to the question that had driven me here in the middle of the night in the first place. I began to weep in great choking sobs.

Please, I thought. *Let me find a way to make my father's pain, his grief, release their hold. Let me find a way to help love flourish. Let me understand what it means to mourn.*

I knelt in the pumpkin patch until all my tears were spent, then returned to my bed and slept a dreamless sleep till morning.

"Cendrillon."

There were hands on my shoulders, shaking me awake.

"Cendrillon!"

Swimming up through layers of sleep, I opened startled eyes. Amelie's flushed face was hovering over mine.

"You have to get up. You have to come and see," she said.

"What is it?" I asked, as I struggled to sit up. "What's wrong?"

"Where is she? Is she coming?" hissed a voice outside my door. I sat bolt upright then.

"Is that Anastasia?"

"Get dressed and be quick about it," Amelie said. "We'll wait for you downstairs. Don't be long."

She dashed from my room. I tossed back the sheets and fumbled into my clothes. I pinned my braids up with trembling fingers, then raced downstairs.

"What is it?" I asked when I reached the great hall. Amelie and Anastasia were standing, hands clasped tightly together, just inside the front door. Without a single word, Amelie grabbed my hand and the two of them tugged me outside.

"Amelie, please, tell me what it is," I begged. "What's wrong?"

"Nothing's wrong," Anastasia snapped, and I actually felt a trickle of relief at her tone. At least she was sounding like her usual self. Hands still linked, we rounded the corner of the house. The early-morning sun smiled down on the kitchen garden.

"We just don't understand what it means, that's all," she went on. "And we want to, before we go and fetch Maman."

"Understand what *what* means?" I asked.

"There," Amelie said, pointing. "In the pumpkin patch."

I skidded to a stop. Together, the three of us stood and stared. The pumpkins were no longer green, still working to ripen, for it was only August. Instead, they glowed like the sun as it sinks into the sea, a hot and vivid orange. And growing up between

the rows, taller than a tall man's head, their brown-and-golden
faces already turning toward the sun, was something I knew
quite well had not been there the night before.

Sunflowers.

They grew an inch a day, till they were as long as the back of
our tallest horse, and then the saplings in our orchards. Blue-
birds came from miles around to flutter around the sunflowers'
brown-and-golden heads. Squirrels climbed up the stalks and
sat upon them, turning them into stools and dinner plates all
at the same time.

My stepmother brought great armfuls of flowers into the
house every day, till the very stones themselves seemed suffused
with a golden glow. Each time she cut a plant down, another
sprang up overnight to take its place. For the first time since
they had arrived, I heard Anastasia laugh, saw my stepmother
smile not just with her face, but with her eyes. In my heart, I
felt a strange new plant take root: hope.

My father had shed no tears, and on the grave of my mother
not a plant would thrive. But I had wept, and with my tears
I had brought something to life that had never been seen on
the grounds of the great stone house before. I still could not
quite see the way for it to happen, but, with the coming of the
sunflowers, I began to believe that all might yet be well. Old
Mathilde was right. Love was all around me. I simply had to
find a way to make it thrive.

"Well, I am off," Amelie's voice suddenly broke into my thoughts, as she appeared at the kitchen door. She came into the room, took a basket Old Mathilde had woven from willow branches down from its hook, and settled it into the crook of one arm.

"Where to today?" I inquired.

Ever since the appearance of the sunflowers, Amelie had given up her fancy dresses entirely. She could have been mistaken for a servant just as easily as I had been. In her plain homespun dress, her sun hat firmly upon her head at her mother's insistence, she had taken her explorations out of doors. With every layer of finery Amelie had shed, it seemed to me that a barrier between us had been shed as well. She did not quite treat me as an equal. We had not come so far as that. But she did not quite treat me like I wasn't, either.

"I am going to the beach," she said, giving the basket a little swing. "Raoul says there are stairs."

I made a face. "There are. Endless ones."

"No matter," Amelie said cheerfully. "As long as they go both up and down."

She moved to the door that led outside and stepped through it.

"Amelie," I said. "May I ask you something?" She turned back, the bright morning sun behind her shadowing her face but glancing off her hair like a halo.

"Of course you may, Cendrillon," she replied.

"What are you looking for?"

I sensed, rather than saw, the way she made a face. "You have to promise not to tell me it's impossible," she said.

"I'll tell you what Old Mathilde would say if she heard you say that," I replied. "She would say that nothing is truly impossible. It's all a matter of looking at things in just the right way."

"That's it!" Amelie cried. "Though I suppose I should say it's a matter of looking *for* things in just the right way.

"I am looking for the thing that cannot be found by searching for it," she said. "The thing Niccolo found, that made him wish to return. I am looking for a surprise."

Ten

THE WEATHER STAYED FINE ALL THROUGH AUGUST, AND THEN September arrived. And with it, though our days were no less pleasant, a certain sense of urgency took up residence in the great stone house. September is a changeable sort of month. One foot in summer and the other in autumn. And if autumn was coming, then winter would not be far behind. It didn't take a fortune-teller to figure out that my stepmother and stepsisters were not looking forward to a winter in a stone house overlooking a cold gray sea.

Anastasia didn't laugh anymore. Instead, she became more exacting than ever, as if determined to make up for lost time. *"Fetch me my slippers, Cendrillon. No not the yellow ones, you stupid girl."* (Though these were the ones that matched her dress.) *"The blue ones. Bring me my shawl. Can't you see that I am cold?"*

For days on end, she kept me running to do her bidding so often I began to fear the soles of my shoes would wear out. Then, one morning, the very same one on which Amelie announced she had at long last finished her explorations at the beach and would spend her day in the peach orchard instead, Anastasia declared her desire to go riding.

"Riding," Raoul exclaimed in disgust when I went to the stable to bring him the news. He was pitching fresh hay into the horses' stalls, spreading it with the tines of a pitchfork. "And my presence is requested, I suppose."

"Not by Anastasia," I answered. "But by her mother. It's not unreasonable, Raoul. No high-born lady would ride without a groom, and Anastasia doesn't know where she is going."

Raoul gave a snort. "That's true enough, in more ways than one." He spread a final forkful of hay. "Who does Chantal de Saint-Andre expect will do my work while I'm babysitting her daughter?"

"I don't imagine she thinks of it quite like that," I said.

This time, Raoul gave a sigh.

"Amelie is not so bad," he admitted, as he returned the pitchfork to its proper place. "If nothing else, she is comfortable with being quiet. But something tells me looking after Miss High-and-Mighty will be a different matter altogether."

"Don't think of it as looking after her, then," I suggested. "Think of it as looking after the horse."

Raoul laughed, then looped an arm around my shoulders. "An excellent suggestion," he admitted, as he brushed his knuckles across the top of my head. "I will do my best to follow it."

"Cendrillon!" Anastasia's imperious voice called. "Why can I never find you when I need you? Where are you? I'm ready to go."

Raoul rolled his eyes, but I could see the wariness that crept into their expression, the way his mouth thinned and tightened at the sound of Anastasia's voice.

"You could always try not saying much," I suggested in a low voice. "It drives her crazy when she can't get a rise out of me." I stepped out of his hold. "I'm in the stable, Anastasia," I called, lifting my voice.

"Where else would you be?" Raoul murmured, but he went to fetch and saddle the horses.

Anastasia was standing in the courtyard, her hands on her hips, wearing the riding habit I had spent most of the morning preparing to her satisfaction. Never, or so it seemed to me, had she looked more lovely. The fabric of the habit was a deep and lustrous blue. In her pale face, her blue eyes blazed like sapphires. She was tapping one booted foot upon the cobblestones with impatience.

"I am ready to go," she said again. "How long does it take that silly stable boy to saddle two horses?"

"If you think he's so silly, I wonder that you feel safe riding out with him," I couldn't quite resist saying, and saw the way she flushed.

"Thank you for your concern," she said tartly.

She continued to tap her foot as the minutes went by, the tempo accelerating the longer we stood in the courtyard. She caught her lower lip between her teeth, shooting anxious glances toward the stable.

She is nervous, I realized suddenly.

Before I had time to consider what that might mean, Raoul appeared, leading two horses. One, the tall black he preferred now that he'd given the dappled gray to Niccolo, and a mare the color of honey. Both were neatly saddled, their coats brushed to a glossy shine. He'd brushed his own hair as well, I noticed.

Anastasia's color rose a little higher, but her voice stayed as sharp as always.

"There you are. It's about time."

For a fraction of a second, I thought Raoul would answer back. I could almost see him bite the inside of one cheek to hold in the smart reply. Then, in a move so unexpected both Anastasia and I blinked, he sketched a quick but perfectly acceptable bow.

"I am at your service, lady," he said, as he straightened up. And then he smiled. Anastasia caught her breath with an audible sound. She opened her mouth, then closed it again. "I'm ready to go whenever you are," Raoul went on sweetly. "But perhaps you've changed your mind."

I bit the inside of my own cheek now, for it seemed to me I understood. He was going to drive Anastasia mad with kindness. Be so attentive she couldn't possibly complain.

I saw her give a little shake, as if snapping herself out of a dream. "Of course I haven't changed my mind," she said. "Help me to mount."

Without a backward glance, she began to march smartly toward the riding block, the small raised platform a lady might use to mount her horse more easily. I expected Raoul to bring the mare to her. He stayed right where he was. When she realized he wasn't moving, Anastasia stopped and turned around. She put her hands on her hips and glared. His face expressionless, Raoul gazed back.

He is daring her to come to him, I realized.

At first it seemed she wouldn't do it. Then, with a lift of her chin, Anastasia took up the challenge. She closed the distance between them with brisk, rapid steps. Raoul bent at the waist, and linked his hands together to form a stirrup. Anastasia placed the toe of her soft leather riding boot between his hands, rested one of her own hands on Raoul's shoulder for balance.

In the next moment, Raoul straightened, and, graceful as a bird, Anastasia went flying upward. She landed in the saddle in a flurry of dark blue skirts. She hooked one knee over the pommel on her lady's riding saddle, gathered the reins into her gloved hands.

"Thank you," she said.

"You are more than welcome."

I stared, not sure which of them had astonished me more. It was the first time I had heard Anastasia say thank you for anything. Raoul sounded polite as a lord. Then, as if to make absolutely certain it was clear who was in charge, Anastasia rapped her heels smartly against the mare's sides, putting her in motion. Raoul had to step back quickly to avoid being stomped on.

"I don't like to be kept waiting," Anastasia announced, even as Raoul was vaulting into his own saddle. "Do try to keep up."

They were gone the whole afternoon, as the weather changed, turning thick and sultry and still, a ring of clouds creeping in from the edges of the sky.

"Thunderstorm weather," Susanne announced with a click of her tongue. "You mark my words, there'll be a storm before the night is out."

By late afternoon I was fractious and edgy, as if my clothes had suddenly grown too tight. Amelie came home from the peach orchard without her sun hat, her face flushed. Chantal lost her temper and gave her a scolding. Amelie went upstairs and did not come back down. After that, my stepmother took to pacing back and forth in the great hall, opening the front door as if she heard Anastasia returning, then closing it again on no one. I often swept the great hall at this time of day, and once a week I scrubbed the flagstones. But it was apparent I would get no work done on this particular afternoon.

"Raoul would never let anything happen to her," I finally volunteered, worn out by my stepmother's pacing as if I had been doing it right alongside her. "He's the best horseman in the county. And he knows every inch of de Brabant lands. He would never let Anastasia come to any harm."

Chantal de Saint-Andre started, as if she'd forgotten I was there.

"Gracious, Cendrillon," she said. "You startled me. And it isn't that I'm worried, it's just . . ." She broke off, raising a hand to her forehead, as if to brush away unwelcome thoughts.

"I am so edgy today. Everything about this place still feels so foreign and wild, and Anastasia can be so headstrong. She's always been that way, ever since she was a child. But since we came here, I . . ." She shook her head, as if to clear it. "All day long, I have felt afraid without quite knowing why. I know it's foolish but . . ."

She broke off as we both heard the clatter of hooves. My stepmother was at the door almost before I could blink, flinging it open wide. She dashed out onto the steps, with me close behind her, just as Anastasia swept into the courtyard.

Gone was the prim and proper maiden who had departed just that morning. In her place was a young woman with her emotions barely under control. Anastasia's long dark hair had come unbound to stream across her shoulders and down her back like an inky waterfall. Her eyes were enormous. The color in her cheeks was high. It was clear that something had happened, and that it had affected her deeply. The question was, what?

She brought the mare to a quick and sudden stop just as Raoul cantered in behind her, his own face the match of the threatening thunderclouds overhead. He dismounted quickly, moved to where Anastasia sat, still as a marble statue on her horse.

"Not you," Anastasia said, her voice slightly breathless. "Go get someone else. I do not want you to touch me."

"My touch is no different than it was a few moments ago," Raoul answered, his voice cracking with temper and something that ran deeper, a thing I could not quite identify. "Besides, there isn't anyone else and you know it. Why must you always behave like a spoiled child?"

Anastasia's flushed cheeks paled. She pressed her lips together, looped her reins over the pommel, and leaned down. She braced herself on Raoul's shoulders as he reached up and swept her from the saddle so swiftly that her long dark hair tumbled forward over her shoulder to stream across his own, obscuring both their faces for the time it took Raoul to set her on her feet. Then Anastasia stepped back, brushing her hair from her face with a fierce gesture.

"Anastasia," said her mother, as she moved down the steps. "Thank goodness you are home."

"Oh, Maman," Anastasia said. She turned away from Raoul, but her long hair would not quite release its hold. It clung to his shirt, like a sweetheart not ready to be parted from him. Raoul turned away, lifting a hand to brush it aside.

"Maman," Anastasia said once more, and I heard the way her voice broke.

"Heavens," her mother exclaimed, as she reached her. "What is it, my child?"

"Nothing. It is nothing," Anastasia said fiercely. "I stayed too long in the sun, that's all. And the weather today makes me feel so strange."

"It's because there's a storm coming," her mother said. "It makes us all feel that way." She put an arm around Anastasia's waist, then pressed a hand to her forehead. "Gracious, you are burning up. Come into the house. We'll get you out of these clothes."

"I want you to help me, Maman," Anastasia said, her voice suddenly small and pleading like a child's. "I don't want anyone else. I don't need anyone else. Not anyone."

"But of course I will help you," her mother said. Without another word, she led Anastasia into the house.

Raoul stood beside Anastasia's horse, his eyes gazing straightforward at nothing. I came down the steps till I stood at his side.

"Would you like me to help rub down the horses?" I asked.

Raoul gave a start. "What?"

"Would you like me to help with the horses?" I said once

more, even as I saw something hot and furious flash into Raoul's eyes. By way of answer, he took two steps, hauled me up against him, and pressed his lips to mine.

Raoul's lips felt just as his eyes looked, desperate, angry, wild. His arm around my waist felt like a band of solid iron. I felt the world do two entirely contradictory things at once. Explode wide open. Narrow down. I felt the way Raoul's heart thundered in his chest, heard the echo of its rhythm in my own. And suddenly I understood the sound that it was making.

No, my heart said, even as it pounded more furious than it ever had before. *Not this. Not him. Not this. No. No. No.*

I made a sound, and Raoul let me go.

We stood for a moment, staring at each other, while the wind explored the corners of the courtyard.

"Oh, damn," Raoul said suddenly. "I've made a mess of things, haven't I? I'm sorry, Cendrillon."

I made a second sound now. A strange combination of outrage and laughter.

"You're *sorry*?" I cried. "You kiss me out of the blue and then stand there and tell me that you're sorry? How can you possibly be such a dolt?"

Raoul's face clouded. Seizing the mare's reins, he began to turn her around. "Fine. You don't want an apology, I'll save my breath."

I planted myself in front of him. "You even think about taking another step," I said, "and I swear on my mother's grave I'll break your arm. I don't want an apology, Raoul. What I want is an explanation."

Raoul dropped the reins, put his hands on his hips. "I was trying," he said succinctly, "to avoid a broken heart."

I felt all my exasperation evaporate as suddenly as it had come upon me. "Oh," I said, and somehow, it didn't sound foolish at all. "Anastasia," I said. "It's Anastasia, isn't it?"

Love at first sight, I thought. I wondered why I hadn't recognized the signs for what they were before now.

They had been there in the tight silences between Raoul and Anastasia whenever they met, the compressed lips, the quick glances from the corners of their eyes. Not all love is joyful, particularly when it seems hopeless. She was a noble-born lady, and proud of it. Raoul was a country stable boy.

"What it is," Raoul declared now, as he picked up the reins once more and began to lead the horses into the barn, "is absolutely impossible."

"So it is Anastasia, then," I said. I followed Raoul into the barn. Together, we undid straps, pulled off saddles, began to rub the horses down, working in silence as we had so often before. But this silence was different, as if the memory of the kiss we'd shared still hovered in the air between us. The knowledge of all the things it had been, and the things that it had not.

I suppose every girl wonders who her true love will be. Will it be some handsome stranger, or the boy next door? I can't precisely claim I had dreamed of falling in love with Raoul, but

I would be a liar if I said the possibility had never crossed my mind.

I took the curry brush from its place and began to brush the coat of the mare Anastasia had ridden to a rich and glossy shine.

"How long have you known?"

Raoul remained silent just long enough that I thought he wasn't going to answer.

"Almost from the first moment," he finally replied. "And don't think I haven't tried to talk myself out of it, because I have, every single day since they all arrived." He shot a quick glance in my direction, as if gauging my reaction. "I'm not a complete idiot," he said. "Even if I am a dolt. Just because I can fall in love with Anastasia doesn't mean I believe we can have a future together."

"I'm sorry I called you names," I said. "I was a little . . ." I took a second to ponder the word I wanted. "Annoyed. For future reference, don't ever kiss a girl and then tell her you're sorry that you've done it." I handed him the brush.

"Thank you for the advice," he said. "It comes a little late, but I'll keep it in mind for the future."

"Don't tell me you kissed her, too!" I cried. "Wait a minute. Of course you did. That's why she looked and behaved the way she did when the two of you arrived."

"Yes, I kissed her," Raoul burst out. "She kissed me right back, if you must know. And it doesn't mean a thing. I am no one, and she is noble-born. She may have forgotten it for a moment or two, but she remembered soon enough. Life would have been a lot simpler if it could have been you."

"Oh, Raoul," I said. I stopped brushing the horse, turned, and put my arms around him even though his back was to me. Raoul rested his head against his horse's flank, then pivoted to return the embrace. I felt the warmth of his breath against my throat.

"I suppose you're quite sure that you don't love me?" he inquired after a while.

I thumped a fist against his back. "I love you with all my heart, as you very well know. It's just not the happily-ever-after kind of love. I apologize if I've ruined all your plans."

"*I've* ruined all my plans," Raoul replied. "But there's no help for it. I got myself into this mess. I'll just have to figure out a way to get myself back out of it."

"And just how do you intend to do that?" inquired a new voice. Raoul and I sprang apart. Anastasia was standing at the entrance to the stall.

"Anastasia," Raoul said hoarsely.

"Do not speak to me." She cut him off in a ragged voice. "I did not give you permission to use my name. I did not give you permission to tell me that you loved me. I believed you, fool that I was."

Her voice rose, the tone mimicking and shrill. *"I can't bear this any longer, Anastasia. No matter what I do, I can't get you out of my mind. I think of you when I should be attending to my duties. I dream of you at night."*

She stamped her foot, as if the action might drive Raoul's words away. "And I let what you said turn my head. It was so surprising, so eloquent for a stable boy. Now I see the reason you're so good at fine words. You've been practicing on Cendrillon."

Before either Raoul or I realized what she intended, Anastasia strode forward and seized me by the arm. "He's kissed you, hasn't he?" she demanded.

"No," I protested. "Not that way."

Anastasia gave my arm a little shake. "You're lying," she said. "I can see it in your eyes."

"He was just trying to prove he didn't love me," I said.

"I don't care if he does love you," Anastasia all but shouted.

With a quick, hard jerk, Anastasia began to tug me out of the stall and toward the stable door. "I don't care if he's always loved you. A stable boy and a kitchen maid. The two of you are perfect for each other. You can live happily ever after for all I care."

We were out in the courtyard now. I felt a sudden gust of wind and the first few drops of rain begin to fall.

"But I will not be made a fool of in my own house."

"It's not your house," Raoul said furiously, as he charged after us. "It's Cendrillon's."

"Raoul," I said. "Stop."

"So she was born in this miserable place," Anastasia flashed out, as she continued to pull me across the courtyard. "What

116

difference does that make? She's still just a servant. She can be dismissed like any other."

We reached the front steps. "Maman!" Anastasia suddenly called out. *"Maman!"*

The front door flew open and Chantal de Saint-Andre dashed out. "What in the world is happening?" she cried. "Anastasia, I thought you were in your room resting. What is wrong?"

"I want you to dismiss Cendrillon," Anastasia said, all but sobbing now. "I will not have her in the house one more moment. I want you to send her away. I demand that you send her away."

"You can't just pack her off like a piece of unwanted baggage," Raoul said hotly.

Anastasia's face went bone white. "Don't you tell me what I can and cannot do," she said. "You are no one. I am a daughter of the house."

Raoul turned to me, and I saw the fury and pain, both bright, in his eyes. "Tell her," he said urgently. "Tell them both right now. If you don't do it, then I will."

"Tell us what, if you please?" Chantal de Saint-Andre said in a firm yet quiet tone. She came partway down the steps. "Do not fear to speak, Cendrillon. I don't understand what is happening, but I do know you have the right to speak, to defend yourself."

"I don't need to be defended," I answered. "For I have done nothing wrong."

"Then speak because I ask you to," she said. "What is being hidden that should be told?"

I lifted my chin, and met my stepmother's eyes.

"I am not a servant, to be sent away on a whim," I said. "I am Etienne de Brabant's daughter."

Eleven

ABSOLUTE SILENCE FILLED THE COURTYARD. IT SEEMED TO ME that even the wind stopped blowing. The rain held off, as if uncertain where to fall. Only my stepmother's gaze remained steady, her eyes looking straight into mine.

Then, utterly without warning, Anastasia moved. She released my arm. But only so she could raise her hand to slap me smartly across the face.

"*Liar!*" she cried.

"Anastasia," her mother's voice cracked like a whip. "That is quite enough." She walked down the remaining steps that separated her from Anastasia, Raoul, and me. Over her shoulder, I saw Amelie skitter out onto the front porch.

"You must never strike another, not even in anger," Chantal de Saint-Andre went on. "Now, calm down, all of you, and tell me what this is all about."

"I caught them together in the stable, Maman," Anastasia hurried into speech. "They had their arms around each other. I won't have that kind of behavior. *I will not have it.* I want them both dismissed at once."

"You can't dismiss either of us," I said. "This is as much Raoul's house as it is mine. He is forbidden to leave de Brabant lands by my father's own order."

"How is it possible," Chantal de Saint-Andre said, "that Etienne de Brabant is your father and I know nothing about it? Is there anyone else who can vouch for the truth of what you say?"

"There is Old Mathilde," I replied. "She delivered me."

"And who was your mother?" Anastasia sneered. "Some local peasant girl, perhaps?"

"My mother was Constanze d'Este," I replied, and as I spoke the words, I felt a burden lift from my heart. My father might never claim me, but here, in this moment, I had finally claimed my mother for my own.

Anastasia's face went white to the lips, and her mother's dark eyes grew wide.

"I have heard that name," Chantal de Saint-Andre said softly. "There were whispers of it at court, the day Etienne and I took our vows. Constanze d'Este, whose beauty had no equal, who died young. But not one whisper that she died bringing a child into the world. Why did your father not tell me of you himself?"

"Because he wishes I had never been born. My father has never forgiven me for taking my mother out of the world by coming into it. He has never acknowledged me, not to anyone outside this house."

"I don't care what you say, I don't believe you," Anastasia declared. "It's a touching story, I must admit, but how do we know it's not a pack of lies?"

"Because Cendrillon looks just like her mother," Amelie said, speaking for the very first time. Her mother and sister swung around.

"How can you know that?" Chantal demanded. "Constanze d'Este died before you were born."

"I have seen her portrait," Amelie answered simply. "It's in the room at the end of the hall, the one that's been locked ever since we arrived. I found the key just this morning, in the peach orchard."

"The peach orchard," my stepmother echoed in a dazed voice.

Amelie came down the steps, her dark eyes both thoughtful and excited as they met mine.

"I got hungry, so I picked a peach," she went on. "Instead of a pit, there was a key inside. I remembered what you had told me, Cendrillon. That Etienne de Brabant was so heartbroken after the death of his first wife that he locked the door to her room, and threw away the key."

"And you found it inside a peach?" Anastasia exclaimed, her tone scoffing. "That's not possible and you know it. You've been out in the sun too long."

"Sunflowers shouldn't have been possible, either," Amelie replied. "But you and Maman picked armloads of those. I searched for something, and I found it."

"Your surprise," I said. "You found your surprise."

Amelie nodded. "A greater one than even I knew to hope for. That day in the hall, why didn't you tell me you were Constanze d'Este and Etienne de Brabant's daughter?"

"I wanted to," I said. "But I didn't know how." I let my gaze take in Chantal and Anastasia. "I didn't know how to tell any of you. I'm sorry. I never meant to make things worse than they already are."

Amelie put a hand into the pocket of the apron she had taken to wearing. She pulled it out to reveal a key resting in the center of her palm.

"I would have let you be the first to open the door," she said, as she held it out toward me. "But I didn't know I should, Cendrillon. Not until I saw the portrait. After that, I came to find everyone. I was about halfway down the stairs when I heard Anastasia bellowing."

Anastasia sucked in a breath. But her mother spoke before she could reply. "I will see this portrait," she said. "And then we will decide what is to be done."

* * *

"I didn't like the thought of locking the room back up again," Amelie said when the four of us arrived outside my mother's door. My stepmother had dispatched Raoul to find Old Mathilde. "But it didn't seem right to just leave the door standing open, so I closed it again."

"Open it, please, Cendrillon," my stepmother said quietly.

I put my hand on the latch, squeezed to lift it upward. I heard the sharp *click* as the catch released. Slowly, as if the hinges couldn't quite remember what it was they were supposed to do, the door to my mother's room swung open.

Great ropes of cobwebs hung down from the ceiling, swaying gently in the sudden movement of the air. The path of Amelie's footprints was plain upon the dusty floor. Moving from the doorway to the far corner of the room, disappearing around a wall which formed an alcove. On the wall closest to us stood a great four-poster bed, its hangings gray with dust. A straight-backed chair sat before the window closest to the bed.

Old Mathilde's chair, I thought.

"Where is the portrait?" I asked, and my own voice sounded as dry as the dust.

"In the alcove," Amelie said.

I took a breath, and stepped across the threshold.

It was no more than fifteen paces from the doorway to the place where the portrait of my mother, Constanze d'Este, still hung upon the wall. Fifteen paces, one for every year that I had been alive. But, then as now, that walk across my mother's room seemed set apart from time. I may be walking across that room still, for all I know. Still making the journey from the doorway to my first glimpse of the face of the woman who had given up her life the night she gave me the gift of mine.

I reached the edge of the alcove, turned the corner, and suddenly I was face-to-face with a woman with hair the color of leaves in autumn, eyes the color of a fresh spring lawn. High cheekbones, pointed chin, a firm and determined mouth. But none of these were the things which brought the fierce and sudden rush of tears to my eyes. The thing that did that was a complete and utter surprise.

"Oh, come and see," I heard my own voice say. "Come and see what love looks like."

Quietly, their footsteps stirring up the dust, Chantal de Saint-Andre and her daughters came to stand at my side. I heard my stepmother catch her breath, and as she did, my tears began to fall.

For never had I seen an expression such as the one that gazed out at us from my mother's portrait. Never had I seen any face so filled with light, with such a pure and radiant joy. There could be only one reason for a look like that, just one cause: looking into the face of the person you loved best in all the world, and finding what you felt reflected back. For the thing that was in my mother's face, shining out from it like a torch in the night, was love.

"Oh, but it is wicked," I suddenly heard my stepmother say, and I barely recognized the sound of her voice. "So terribly wicked, to be given such a gift and throw it all away. So terribly, terribly wrong."

"Maman, what is it? What's the matter?" I heard Amelie exclaim. "Maman!"

I turned my head, then, to look at my stepmother, and found to my astonishment that Chantal de Saint-Andre was weeping also. Huge tears streamed down her face to stain the silk of her gown. The ice inside her was well and truly melted now.

"I have been such a fool!" she cried. "I should have had this door broken down the very day that I arrived. I have behaved no better than your father, Cendrillon. I was so certain I had been betrayed by the one I trusted most of all. So furious with the king for making me marry your father that I forgot the reason I'd given him my trust in the first place. I forgot about love."

She turned to face me then, and I saw that her tears were already beginning to dry. In her face was a light that I had never seen before.

"But here love is," Chantal de Saint-Andre said. "Shining out from your mother's face, locked up, hidden away for all this time. I look at it, and I feel ashamed, for your betrayal is much greater than mine has ever been, Cendrillon. Your father threw away the greatest gift your mother could bestow—the gift of what their love created. I think that I have never heard of anything so wrongheaded, or so blind."

"I wished for you," I heard myself say. "A mother to love me, a mother I might love. And two sisters in the bargain."

"Why two?" Anastasia asked at once.

"So that at least one of them might like me," I said.

Before I knew quite what she intended, Chantal stepped forward. She slipped the kerchief from my head, unpinned my braids so that they tumbled down. Then she untied the scraps of fabric at the ends of my hair, and with her quick, gentle fingers, combed out the braids until my hair lay thick and unbound across my shoulders, flowing down my back till its ends tickled the backs of my knees.

Then she turned me, her touch still gentle, to once again face my mother's portrait.

"I cannot claim that I can be the mother she would have been," Chantal de Saint-Andre said quietly. "In this moment, I cannot even claim to love you, Cendrillon, for to truly love takes seeing truly, and I am seeing you now for the very first time.

"But I can promise you that I will try. Let there be no more throwing away of love while I am mistress of this house."

"I don't know what to say to you," I said.

"It's simple enough," Anastasia said. "You say, 'Thank you, Maman.'"

"Oh, there you are!" her mother said to her. "There is the

daughter that I know and love. I knew you could not have lost yourself forever." She turned me to face her now, gathering us both, and Amelie, too, into her arms. "Another daughter," she said. "What a wonderful gift."

"Thank you," I said. "Thank you, Maman."

Twelve

I SLEPT A DEEP AND DREAMLESS SLEEP THAT NIGHT, AND IN the morning awoke to yet another series of surprises. The first was that my stepmother and Old Mathilde had put their heads together and decided that I was to be treated like a servant no longer. Instead, I was to take my place as what I truly was: a daughter of the house. With that in mind, my stepmother escorted me into breakfast herself. Seated at the table was the second surprise.

"Niccolo!" I cried. "When did you arrive?"

He got to his feet at once, made me a perfect court bow, then swept me up into a hug.

"Late last night," he replied. "I didn't want to wake the

house, so I roused Raoul in the stable instead. Somehow, I knew that's where I'd find him."

And where he would remain as much as possible, I thought, as I returned Niccolo's embrace, then let him go. My status in the great stone house might have changed overnight, but Raoul's was still the same as always.

"I thought I brought important news," Niccolo went on as he pulled out a chair for me. I took it, feeling more than a little self-conscious. "But *your* news, little Cendrillon . . ."

"Why does everyone insist on calling me little?" I said. "I'm just as tall as Amelie."

Niccolo helped my stepmother to the chair at the head of the table, then took a place beside me. He and I were on one side of the table, Amelie and Anastasia on the other. Niccolo shot a quick glance in Amelie's direction, then cocked his head in a perfect imitation of her. I heard Chantal chuckle. She made a gesture, and the village girl waiting by the table began to serve the breakfast.

"He has captured you, Amelie," observed her mother.

Amelie lifted her chin, her eyes gazing straight into Niccolo's. I saw the way they sparkled. Then she cocked her head in the opposite direction of the one that he had chosen. I bit down on my tongue to keep from laughing, and even Anastasia smiled.

"Has he?" Amelie inquired. "I can't imagine why you would say such a thing."

"No?" Niccolo said, as he tilted his head to the other side. Slowly, her eyes still holding his, Amelie tilted her head in the opposite direction.

"No."

Niccolo laughed aloud. "You are too clever for me, lady Amelie," he said. "In the future, I will make certain to keep that in mind."

"Oh, I don't know," Amelie replied, her eyes on her own hands as she added some of Old Mathilde's blackberry jam to a piece of buttered toast. "I would have thought we were pretty well matched."

"*Amelie*," Anastasia said, scandalized.

Amelie lifted her eyes. The expression in them was absolutely guileless. "What?" she asked. From the corner of my eye, I thought I saw her mother smile.

So that is the way of things, I realized. I flicked a glance in Niccolo's direction and found him industriously studying his napkin. *They will make a good pair,* I thought. Amelie's inquisitive nature and Niccolo's open one. And I had to admit, he did look well. His cheeks were tanned from whatever journeys he had undertaken in the summer months. He had a fine new suit of clothes. *He looks like what he is now,* I thought suddenly. *A nobleman's son, even if a younger one.*

Anastasia cleared her throat. "You said you had news from court, Niccolo," she said. "Will you tell us?"

"But of course," Niccolo answered, and there was both

excitement and a note of something deeper in his eyes. "The news I come with is this: The prince has returned to the court."

"Prince Pascal? I have not seen him since he was a small boy," my stepmother said.

"Surely you have seen the prince, Niccolo." Anastasia said, her voice eager. "Tell us what he is like."

"Ah!" Niccolo said, and now his eyes were dancing with mischief. "Here, I fear I must disappoint you. It is true that I have seen the prince, but equally true that I can tell you almost nothing about him save what everybody knows."

"There is some story in this, I think," I said over my stepsisters' exclamations of dismay.

Niccolo nodded. "There is, and I will tell it if you will but give me a moment."

"Be quiet, Amelie," Anastasia said at once. I bit down hard on the tip of my tongue.

"The prince is much away from court," Niccolo explained by way of a beginning. "This has been so for many years, ever since the Prince Pascal was little more than a boy. His travels served as a way for him to learn all the corners of his land and the people he will rule someday."

"Not to mention keeping him outside his mother's influence," Amelie observed.

Niccolo gave a quick nod. "That is so," he acknowledged. "In this, the cleverness of the king is crystal clear, for over the years the bond between the prince and the common people has grown strong. Though he is young, he is just, and loved wherever he goes."

"He sounds boring," Amelie remarked.

"Amelie!" Anastasia exclaimed. "He's a prince."

Amelie turned toward her sister. "Is there some rule that says a young man can't be a handsome prince and a terrible bore all at the same time?"

Anastasia began to sputter. "Pay no attention to them," I advised. "It's what I do. Go on, Niccolo."

"I don't know how things have been here," Niccolo continued, "but in the capital we have had as fine a summer as any could wish for. But the very day the prince was set to return from the journeys that have kept him away all summer long, we had an unexpected thunderstorm. The rain fell thick as blankets, and the raindrops themselves were as big as coins. Fields and roads that had been dry as dust were suddenly filled with nothing but mud."

"That sounds strangely familiar," Anastasia said.

Niccolo chuckled. "I wondered if it might. Not an hour after the rain ceased, the prince and his retainers rode into the palace courtyard. At once, a great hue and cry went up. The king and queen were sent for. Anyone who could dashed to a window to look out.

"The prince and his household were so covered in mud there was only one face among them it was easy to recognize—that of Gaspard Turenne, who has been the prince's principal retainer for many years. The king first set him to serve the prince when Pascal was only a boy. Gaspard Turenne has shoulders as broad as an ox, and sports a great dark beard besides.

"After the grooms had taken the horses, Turenne thought to make himself a bit more presentable by cleaning the mud from his face in a nearby water trough. No sooner did he bend over it, than one of the others snuck up behind him and pushed him in. He came up with a great roar, reached up, and dragged the culprit in beside him."

"Don't tell me," I said. "It was Prince Pascal."

"It was," Niccolo replied with a broad smile, as if he could see the scene before him, even now. "By the time the king and queen finally arrived, there was a full-fledged water fight going on. Every single member of the prince's household was involved. The king laughed so hard tears ran down his face as he embraced both Turenne and his son.

"He put an arm around each, and led them both inside. The others followed, still laughing and joking. They looked for all the world like a pack of sorry, soggy dogs. But I heard a man standing near me say that every single man among them would step between the prince and death without a second thought."

"So he is not boring at all," I observed. "And he inspires devotion in those around him. He sounds as if he will make a fine king someday."

"I believe that he will," Niccolo said. "And it is clear his father does, as well. But that is all the glimpse I had of the prince, I'm sorry to say. He stayed in close conference with his father all that evening. The next morning, all the messengers were sent from court to carry the result of that conference throughout the land. We could not even stay to hear it officially proclaimed, but were ordered to set off at once."

"Hear what proclaimed, Niccolo?" my stepmother asked.

"By order of the king, Prince Pascal will marry," Niccolo answered. "That is what I have come to tell you. And there is more: The prince himself will select his bride. The mourning period for the queen's father will be up in three weeks' time. The day after it is ended, there will be a great ball held in the palace. Every eligible maiden in the kingdom is required to attend. From among them, the prince will choose a bride."

A startled silence filled the dining room. Then my stepmother began to laugh.

"Oh, that is well done. No foreign princess to complicate matters by creating yet another alliance. Instead, the prince will marry one of his own. The queen must be beside herself with fury. She will perceive it as a slight that her son should marry a subject, no matter how high-born."

"You are right about that, I think," Niccolo said. "Though of course she has made no protest in public."

"And Prince Pascal?" I asked. "What does he think about it?"

"Nobody knows for certain," Niccolo said. "To be perfectly honest, I don't think it would occur to anyone to ask. He is a prince. It is his duty to marry, and he'll have more choice in the matter than his father ever did."

"But don't you see what this means?" Anastasia broke in excitedly. "It means we can leave this place at last. We can go to court. Indeed, we must. Every eligible maiden is ordered to attend."

Impulsively, she leaned forward to grip Amelie by the hand. "That means us!"

"Indeed it does," Amelie said. "And Cendrillon, too, of course."

Anastasia's face went blank. "That is what I meant," she said. "Cendrillon, too, of course."

"There's no need for me to go," I said quickly. "I have no desire to see the court." Just the thought of it made a strange cold hole in the pit of my stomach. My father, the father I had never seen, who had never wished to see me, had spent his whole life at court.

"It is the king's command," my stepmother replied in a thoughtful voice. "The fact that you've been overlooked for all these years doesn't change the fact that you are noble-born." She drummed her fingertips upon the tabletop. "When is this ball to be, did you say?"

"In mid-October," Niccolo said. "Not quite three weeks' time."

My stepmother stood up abruptly. "In that case, we have no time to waste," she said smartly. "Come along, my girls. We have work to do." She strode toward the doorway, then turned back, a smile dancing at the edges of her mouth.

"I mean you, too, my little Cendrillon."

"No, no, take small steps, *small steps,*" Anastasia exclaimed in irritation several days later. "How many times must you be reminded? You are a young lady walking into a roomful of eager suitors, not a milkmaid striding into a barn."

"I'll bet the milkmaid's shoes are more comfortable," I said, as I finally managed to get across the room and flop down onto a couch. "These pinch."

"That's good," Anastasia said. "They're supposed to. It will remind you to slow down."

A week had passed since Niccolo's return. One solid week of torture. At my stepmother's instigation, and with Old Mathilde's full approval, a campaign was underway to make a proper young lady of me before we set out for court. Even Anastasia had embraced the plan with enthusiasm. Secretly, I believed it had to do with the fact that transforming me into a lady opened up whole new realms of possibilities when it came to ordering me around.

"Sit up straight, Cendrillon," Anastasia said now. "You're slumping. A young lady always keeps her back straight, and her feet tucked neatly underneath her skirts."

I glared at where she sat in a straight-backed chair across the room, effortlessly demonstrating the desired posture.

"Do you never get tired of giving orders?" I inquired. "Amelie must be around somewhere. Why not go pick on her for a change?"

"Because Amelie knows how to behave like a lady when she wants to," Anastasia replied serenely. "Whereas you do not."

"I know part of it involves being polite," I came right back. "Apparently, you missed that part."

Anastasia made a disparaging sound, but I thought I caught a glimpse of a smile at the corners of her mouth. The truth is, I think she was beginning to enjoy our sparring. Now that we were of equal rank, I made a more worthy and interesting opponent.

"Do you want to make a good impression on the prince or not?" she inquired.

"There are going to be hundreds of girls at the ball," I said. "I'm hardly likely to make any impression at all, among so many of them."

Anastasia cocked her head in a perfect imitation of Amelie, her eyes thoughtful now. "You are wrong about that, I think," she said in a voice that matched her eyes. "Much as I hate to admit it, you really are incredibly lovely, Cendrillon."

I sat up a little straighter, as if she'd poked me with a pin.

"That's it," Anastasia exclaimed in delight. "Keep your back just like that."

"You and Amelie are beautiful," I protested.

"I never said we weren't," Anastasia replied. "Cross your

ankles and keep your legs beneath your skirts." I complied.
"Now clasp your hands loosely and place them in your lap." I
did this, too, and actually won a smile.

"That's absolutely perfect," Anastasia said. She regarded me
for a moment, as if trying to decide whether or not to go on.
"There will be many dark-haired girls at court. Some will have
blue eyes, and some brown. But if there's another one who
looks like you among them, I'll eat my riding gloves."

I held my body still, trying to understand what sitting like a
lady felt like. "Would you marry the prince, if he asked you to?"

Surprise flickered over Anastasia's features. "Of course."

"Even though you don't love him, nor he you?"

Anastasia lifted an eyebrow. "You think I am unlovable?"

"I didn't say that," I replied. *Raoul loves you,* I thought, but
didn't quite dare to say aloud. "It's just—don't you want to
marry for love?"

"Of course I do," Anastasia said simply. "Isn't that what every
girl dreams of? But noble-born girls do not always have the
luxury of having their wishes come true."

"You don't have to be noble-born to be disappointed," I
said.

Anastasia nodded. "True enough."

We sat silently for a moment, my gaze on her, her gaze on
nothing.

"About Raoul," I said, taking courage firmly between both
loosely clasped ladylike hands.

"Oh, no," Anastasia said suddenly. "Please, don't."

"There is nothing between us," I said. "Nothing that could stand in the way of him loving someone else."

"Why are you being so nice to me?" Anastasia cried out suddenly. "I've done nothing but torment you since the day I arrived. And yet there you sit, as good as telling me that Raoul can be mine. He can't be, and we all know it. I am a nobleman's daughter, and he's a stable boy. That sort of arrangement may work out well in stories and in dreams. But not in real life."

"No one knows who Raoul really is," I said. "Not even Raoul himself. My father brought him here when he was just two weeks old. Did you not know this?"

"No," Anastasia whispered, her cheeks pale. "No, I did not. Why has no one spoken of this before?"

"Because the subject pains him," I said, and prayed Raoul would not think that I was betraying his confidence. "And there may be no sense in getting your hopes up. He may turn out to be nothing more than what you see right now. Or his origins may always remain a mystery, though I hope that they do not, for learning who he truly is has always been the first wish of his heart.

"I do know this much, though. If I were you, I'd go take a good look at my mother's portrait before I decided to throw away a chance at love."

Anastasia drew a shaky breath. "I do believe," she said, "that this is your attempt to order me around."

I laughed before I quite realized what I'd done. "Perhaps you're right," I acknowledged.

"I will think about what you've said," Anastasia promised. She clapped her hands together sharply. "Now. Let me see you walk across the room one more time. If you do it to my satisfaction, I'll let you put on those terrible gardening clogs."

"At least they don't pinch," I said, as I got to my feet. But before I could so much as take a step forward, Amelie came flying into the room.

"There's been a messenger from Etienne de Brabant," she said breathlessly. "You must both come at once."

Thirteen

THE MESSAGE WAS BRIEF AND TO THE POINT. ALTHOUGH THE king had ordered every eligible maiden in the kingdom to attend the ball in Prince Pascal's honor, Etienne de Brabant was ordering his wife and stepdaughters to stay home.

"He says he fears for your safety," Niccolo said, as he scanned the thick sheet of paper. The messenger who'd brought it was being fed in the kitchen. Raoul was seeing to his horse. My stepmother, stepsisters, Niccolo, and I were in the sun room, the tiny space crowded with so many of us. Pale October sunlight came in through the windows. A fire was kindled in the hearth, for the day was chilly in spite of the light.

"The journey from this place to the court takes several days, and he has heard that there are bandits on all the main roads," Niccolo went on. "A high-born lady and her daughters traveling together would surely attract their attention. Therefore, for your safety and that of your daughters, he commands you to stay at home.

"In your stead, I . . ." Niccolo broke off, his startled eyes rising up from the paper to focus on mine. "In your stead, I am to bring Raoul."

Chantal de Saint-Andre extended a hand. "Thank you, Niccolo," she said. "Please let me see the note."

Niccolo placed it into her hand. As she read the words my father had written, Chantal de Saint-Andre tapped her foot rapidly, to what seemed to me must be the rhythm of her thoughts. Then, with a suddenness that left all of us gasping, she tore the note in two, and then in two once more. Taking three quick steps, she moved to the fireplace.

"What a pity those same bandits set upon my husband's messenger and delayed him," she said serenely, as she cast the scraps of paper upon the fire. "So that the command to keep us all at home did not arrive in time."

"But, Maman, the messenger," Amelie began.

"Will be well cared for and kept busy here till we are well on our way," her mother replied. "He looked as if he could use a little country air, don't you think?"

Her foot began to tap once more. Her dark eyes shone with determination. "I know there are decisions to be made, obstacles to overcome, but we are *not* staying home. It is by the king's command that we are summoned to the palace, and to the palace we shall go. Etienne de Brabant may believe he is my lord and master, but the king is his."

All of a sudden, she gave a grin. "The command of a king trumps that of a husband, every time."

"And Raoul?" I inquired.

Chantal de Saint-Andre's foot stilled.

"Deciding what to do about Raoul," she said, her smile fading away, "may be our very first obstacle. I know that you are close to him, Cendrillon, but I must tell you plainly that the wisest course of action might be to leave Raoul behind. Etienne has always been the queen's man for many years, and I fear some mischief is behind this sudden request. I do not trust this fine husband of mine."

I opened my mouth to protest such a course of action, but before I could speak, my stepmother lifted a hand.

"That is not what I am going to do, however. It would be cruel to leave Raoul at home. Instead, we will all go, including Old Mathilde."

She glanced at Niccolo, who was standing near the fireplace. "The second thing we must decide is what to do about you, Niccolo. If you help us, you will be acting against my husband's wishes, and, for all we know, the queen's as well. Perhaps it is you who should stay here."

Niccolo was silent for a moment. "Thank you, my lady," he

said at last. "Your words are just what I have come to expect, both kind and thoughtful." He looked up from his contemplation of the fire then, and met Amelie's eyes.

"But I think, perhaps, I have done all I can in your husband's service, and in the queen's, if the truth must be told. Since going to court I . . ." He broke off, as if he could not quite put what had happened into words.

He no longer supports the queen, I thought. *And he loves Amelie. He would not wish to do anything which might jeopardize her family.*

"It is time to choose a new allegiance, one more in keeping with the wishes of my own heart," Niccolo went on. He switched his attention back to Chantal. "I will serve you, if you will have me."

"With pleasure," my stepmother replied. "Now all we have to do is find some means of getting to the capital that does not run the risk of alerting my fine and clever husband that we're coming after all. That will mean we cannot take the coach."

"I know," I said suddenly, as the idea sprang, full-blown, into my mind. I could only hope Anastasia was feeling flexible. "Pumpkins."

By the end of the day, a plan had been agreed upon. We would travel as a country family, eager to catch a glimpse of the prince we had never seen, and the lovely young ladies from among whom he would select his bride. To this end, we would harvest our pumpkins, fill the largest wagon with them, and travel to the market in the capital.

"But where will we stay once we get there?" Amelie inquired. "We can hardly put up at an inn, nor can we go to Etienne de Brabant's rooms at court."

"I believe that I can provide a solution to that," Old Mathilde spoke up. We were sitting at the table in the dining room, all of us together, like the family we would soon be impersonating. "I lived in the city, long ago. My sister still lives in the house our parents owned. She will welcome us, and though it will be cozy, there should be room for all."

"You lived in the city?" I exclaimed in astonishment. I had never heard her speak of this before.

Old Mathilde simply smiled and said no more.

"It would seem that you are right, Niccolo," I huffed. "This house is full of surprises."

The journey to the city took three days, days so full of sights and sounds that, though the road we traveled ran straight enough, our path upon it never runs quite the same way twice when I call it to mind. It does not roll out smoothly, like a length of ribbon unfurling across a tabletop, but splinters into different pieces, tumbling all together, then coming together into a single episode, like the spin and halt of a kaleidoscope.

Give one turn and there is Old Mathilde, driving the wagon with Amelie beside her, while Niccolo, dressed like a country lad now, makes his horse prance alongside. He reaches down and, before Amelie quite realizes what he intends, he snatches her up and sets her before him. She throws her arms around his neck to keep from falling off, though even Niccolo knows that this is mostly for show. Amelie is as fine a horsewoman as her sister is. There's not much chance she's going to take a tumble. Niccolo's dark eyes are dancing with mischief. Amelie's cheeks have a rosy glow.

"That looks pretty settled to me," Old Mathilde says, at which my stepmother gives a laugh.

"So it does," she answers. "So it does."

The kaleidoscope gives another turn and I see my stepmother, in the back of the wagon, perched high atop a pile of pumpkins. The wagon hits an unexpected bump in the road. She struggles not to topple out, howling with unrestrained laughter the whole while.

A third twist and Anastasia and Raoul come into view, walking side by side. It is almost twilight, the hour when the day birds are busy finishing up what they have to say before the dark descends and they fall silent for the night. Raoul is teaching Anastasia how to tell which bird is which, for he knows them all by sound alone.

Without warning, the air around us falls silent, and then, into that silence, comes a single bird call. Anastasia stops walking so abruptly Raoul goes several steps beyond her before he even realizes she's no longer beside him.

"Chickadee!" Anastasia cries. "It says its own name when it sings."

Raoul's face splits into a smile. "That's exactly right."

At his words, the bird calls once more, and Anastasia claps her hands together like a small child. "I did it!" she says, spinning toward the wagon. "Did you hear? I did it, Maman!"

And then, at last, the kaleidoscope spins and settles, and we are at the nightfall that followed. One that had us passing through the city gates, our three-day journey almost over.

"My house is in the oldest part of the city," Old Mathilde explained as we began to wind our way through the narrow streets. Mathilde was driving the horse once more. Raoul walked at its head, the better to guide it and keep it calm. Personally, I thought the horse was feeling just as nervous as I was, overwhelmed by the sheer size and complexity of this place to which we had come. Passing through the gate, traveling along the cobblestoned streets, was like entering another country. The narrow streets were bordered by still narrower sidewalks with tall buildings leaning out over all.

"The palace came first, on top of the hill, with the old town directly below it," Old Mathilde went on. "As more people arrived, the town grew down the slopes of the hill."

"It looks like a garden," I said, as we took a turn. "Terraced up the hillside."

Old Mathilde smiled. "That is a good description," she said.

"Well, I think it looks like a crown." Anastasia suddenly spoke up. "All the lights in the windows sparkle like jewels, don't you think?"

"You're just seeing crowns everywhere, now that you're about to meet the prince at last," Amelie teased.

"I am not!" Anastasia cried.

"Girls," their mother said. "It is late, and we are all tired. Let us see if we can make it to our destination without calling attention to ourselves by quarreling in the street, shall we?"

"The lights in the windows are placed there by order of the king," Niccolo supplied into the awkward silence. He had dismounted to lead his horse, as well. He followed along behind the cart. The street was too narrow for us to go abreast.

"Every household must keep a candle burning in each groundfloor window until midnight. After that, the watch patrols the streets, calling out if all is well."

The street took a tight turn, then opened up as we came to an intersection. Niccolo pointed. "Even the palace follows this law. There. You can see it now."

I turned my head, followed the reach of his arm with my eyes, and saw the palace for the very first time. A seemingly impossible collection of turrets, towers, and walls. A light shone from every window on the lower levels, with a smattering of lights twinkling from the floors above.

This is where my father has spent my entire life, I thought.

What would I feel like when I finally set foot inside it? When he finally set eyes upon me, what would be Etienne de Brabant's response?

In the safety of the great stone house, coming to the capital to attend the ball against my father's wishes had seemed the right thing to do, a fine act of rebellion and defiance. But now, gazing up at the palace, I was not so sure. What would it be like to enter the palace as the young noblewoman that I was, to come face-to-face with the father who had neglected me for all my life, with the eyes of countless strangers upon us?

I felt a hard fist of fear begin to form, solid as a snowball, in my gut. Then Old Mathilde clicked to the horse, and the wagon started forward.

"Not much farther now."

Two blocks later, Mathilde brought us to a halt before a house that had a sprig of rosemary and a mortar and pestle painted on a sign hanging over the door. Even in the street, it seemed to me that I could catch a quick aroma of earth, the scent of pungent leaves drying. An apothecary shop. I felt the fist of ice in my belly begin to thaw.

"Your sister is a healer too?" I asked.

Old Mathilde nodded. "As was our mother before us. This was her shop before it was ours. My sister has kept it for us both, while I had other things to do."

She got down from the wagon, handed the reins to Raoul,

then rapped smartly on the door. Only then did I realize we had sent no word of our coming. Before I could express my concern, the door opened. Warm light spilled out into the street, partially cut off as a figure stepped into the doorway.

"I see you are come home at last, Mathilde," a woman's voice said, the sound of it like music. "It's about time."

Old Mathilde's sister was named Justine, and she was a younger, plumper version of Mathilde herself. Her cheeks were pink, and her face as wrinkled as an apple doll's.

"I am afraid the young men must sleep in the stable with the horses," she said, as she made us welcome. The apothecary shop filled the entire downstairs. There were living quarters on the floors above.

"I don't think either of them will mind that," I said. "Raoul sleeps with the horses at home most nights, anyhow."

Justine gave a chuckle. "Then I will leave them to settle themselves," she said. "And after they have done so, they must come in to supper. You young ladies, follow me now."

She led the way upstairs, the rustling of her petticoats beneath her skirts reminding me of the herbs she dried.

"So you are the girl Mathilde has cared for all these years," she said, as she climbed the stairs.

"You know about me?" I asked, astonished. "But how?"

Justine chuckled. "Mathilde and I have our little ways," she said. With that, she threw open a door halfway down the upstairs corridor, then stepped inside. Before us stretched a dormer room that ran the length of the house. Down its center, at regularly spaced intervals, were four neatly made beds, precisely as if they were waiting for us.

"There should be room for all of you in here," Justine said. "The room on the other side gets better light, so we'll save that for the sewing." She turned to my stepmother. "I have taken the liberty of laying in a few things I thought you might find useful," she said. "I hope you don't mind."

"Mind?" my stepmother cried. "You are a lifesaver, Justine, just as your sister is. Part of me wants to ask how you know what to do, the other informs the rest that a gift is best accepted with thanks and not inquired after too closely. So I will simply say thank you, I think. With all my heart."

Justine smiled. "And with all mine, lady, you are most welcome. I will leave you to get settled in, then," she said. "Over supper, we can discuss what must be done."

The rest of that week was a blur of activity, a whirl of fabrics, ribbons, buttons, and pearls. For what seemed like endless hours, Amelie, Anastasia, and I took turns standing in place while Old Mathilde and Justine held up pieces of muslin and made mysterious markings on them. After this we were sent to the kitchen for a cup of tea, but even in that faraway room of the house it seemed to me that I could hear the sound of scissors, swishing and snipping their way through the silks and satins my stepmother had chosen. I went to bed each night with

visions of pins and needles dancing in my head, and any dreams
I had were of thimbles and thread.

Tuesday came and went, then Wednesday, and Friday was
the night of the ball.

"We won't be ready in time," Anastasia declared late Thurs-
day afternoon. "I simply don't see how it can be done. We've
only got so many hands and hours in a day."

"My hands are sewing as fast as they can," I said. I was working on Anastasia's dress, a fine blue silk that matched her eyes,
stitching a smattering of seed pearls across the bodice. With it
would go a circlet of pearls for her forehead, pearl-covered slippers for her feet. Justine was working on Amelie's dress, Chantal
on her own, and Old Mathilde on mine. She would not let me
see it. I didn't even know what color it was.

As the week progressed, Old Mathilde had come to find me
from time to time. She would wrap some body part with a tape
measure, make a note of what she'd learned, then go off again,
muttering instructions to herself.

"That isn't what I meant," Anastasia said. "I do not mean to
criticize. I genuinely do not understand how we can be ready
in time."

"Perhaps it is not a matter for understanding," Amelie put
in. She was weaving together a circlet of dried flowers for her
hair, with a flutter of ribbons that would stream down her back.
"Perhaps it is more along the lines of a wish we all hope may
come true."

"If I were you," I advised, "I would wish and sew at the same time. Hand me that spool of thread, if you please."

But by bedtime, even I began to have my doubts. We worked through the entire length of a brand-new candle, then went to bed with the dresses still undone.

Late that night, I was suddenly awakened by a pair of hands upon my shoulders. Amelie was leaning over my bed, a pale shape in her white nightgown. Anastasia was kneeling at the head of the bed.

"Come into the sewing room," she said. "There is something you should see. But be quiet. We do not want to wake Maman."

I tossed back my covers and got out of bed, following my stepsisters on tiptoe across the hall. In the light of the waning moon, just inside the sewing-room door, two dress forms stood, side by side. One was wearing a dress of pale blue, the other, a pink as soft as inside of a seashell.

"Look," Amelie said. "There we are."

"Oh, but they are perfect," I exclaimed softly. "Perfect in every detail." On silent feet, I moved forward, then knelt to lift the hem of Amelie's dress. "Your hem is finished, Amelie."

She nodded. "And Anastasia's buttons. And look . . ." She gestured to the circlet of flowers she had been working on just that afternoon. Woven in among the blossoms were ropes of tiny seashells. Shell buckles adorned her shoes. In the moonlight, the pearls on Anastasia's dress made the dress glimmer like cool spring rain.

"You are going to be so beautiful," I said, as I stood up. "Both of you."

"Not as beautiful as you will be," Anastasia replied. "Come and see."

"No, wait," Amelie whispered. "Better yet, close your eyes. Don't worry," she went on when I hesitated. "I won't let Anastasia trip you."

"Oh, stop," Anastasia protested, but I caught the laughter in her quiet voice. "She's right, though. Close your eyes, Cendrillon. Please."

Pulling in a deep breath, I obeyed, and felt my stepsisters each clasp a hand. Slowly and carefully, they led me through what felt like the full length of the sewing room.

"Now," Amelie whispered, as she gave my hand a squeeze. "Open your eyes."

I discovered I couldn't quite manage both at once. Instead, I did it one at a time. First the left eye, and then the right. Before me, in a shaft of moonlight coming through the window in the farthest corner of the room, stood the third and final dress form. I blinked. I rubbed my eyes, then blinked again.

"Oh," I said. "Oh, my."

The dress before me was the loveliest that I had ever seen, yard upon yard of ivory-colored satin shot through with threads of gold. The smooth, tight-fitting bodice was embroidered all over with raised gold flowers, their centers brilliants that caught the light. More brilliants danced across the full, billowing skirt.

"It's the same color as the moonlight," Anastasia breathed. "And see—for your hair . . ." She caught up a length of lace as fine as spiderweb, tossed it up and over my head. More brilliants flashed, even in the pale moonlight.

"You will be more beautiful than just the moon," she said. "You will be the moon and the stars combined. We are going to have to resign ourselves to lives as ladies in waiting, Amelie. One look at Cendrillon, and the prince will fall in love at first sight."

"Look," Amelie said. She knelt before the dress form, then rose. "Your slippers are made of glass."

My heart had begun to beat so hard and fast, I feared it would explode. At the sight of the slippers, I put my hands to my mouth.

"What the prince is going to do is die laughing when I fall flat on my face in those. I'm just a country girl, no matter who my mother was. I don't belong in a palace. I can't wear a dress like that."

A dress so beautiful it made my throat ache, so exquisite it made me want to cry. I lifted the lace from my hair, laid it gently against the shoulder of the dress form.

"I'm afraid. I'm so afraid," I whispered.

"It's just for a few hours," Anastasia said softly. "Though remarkable things may happen in even that short amount of time. You surprised us. Perhaps it's time to surprise yourself."

"If I can keep from falling over when I curtsy to the prince,"

I said, "that may be remarkable enough. Now let's go back to bed. It won't matter how beautiful our dresses are if we all have bags under our eyes."

Carefully, Amelie returned my glass slippers to their place. "I still don't understand how all this got done in time," she said, as she rose. "Is it magic, do you suppose?"

"The strongest kind there is, I think," I said.

"And what is that?" Anastasia asked.

"Love."

Fourteen

THE DAY OF THE BALL DAWNED CLEAR AND FINE. WE AROSE TO
eat a hearty breakfast, after which Old Mathilde herded us
into the bath, one by one. Then she sent us to the sunniest
room in the house to comb out our hair and let it dry. Niccolo and Raoul went out into the city to make the arrange-
ments for the coach that would take us to the palace that
night. They had been whispering and chuckling together ever
since the day before. If Susanne had been with us, she'd have
called them thick as thieves. It was clear that they were up to
something.

Late in the afternoon, there came a sudden lull in our
activities, like the calm before the storm. My stepsisters and

I were in our room, sitting in a circle with our backs to one another. I brushed Anastasia's hair, Anastasia Amelie's, and Amelie mine.

"What happens if they can't find a carriage?" Anastasia suddenly said. "We can't go in the wagon and we can't possibly walk. Those shoes are gorgeous, but they hurt my feet. Ouch, Cendrillon. You're pulling my hair!"

"I'm not," I replied. "Stop fussing, Anastasia. Raoul and Niccolo know what they're about."

As if summoned by our words, we heard a shout from the street below. I heard my stepmother begin to laugh.

"Oh, it is absolutely perfect," she cried. "I could not have done better if I'd chosen it myself."

Anastasia flew to the window, opening the casement so that she could lean out. A moment later, I heard her laugh too.

"Oh, do come look!" she cried.

Amelie and I crowded into the window so that we all three together gazed down into the street below. Raoul sat behind two fine new horses, hitched to a conveyance, the likes of which I had never seen before. It had tall, thin wheels with spokes of painted gold. The coachman's seat was perched so high it was a wonder Raoul didn't fall right off. But the carriage itself was the most astonishing sight of all. Great and round, with great round windows to match. Like the wheels, it was painted gold.

"How do you like it?" Raoul called up with a doff of his new hat. He looked like a fine gentleman in his recently acquired city clothes. He and Niccolo would drive us to the palace that night.

"Leave it to you," Anastasia said, "to find the only carriage in all the city that looks exactly like a pumpkin."

Anastasia, Amelie, and I dressed together, aided by Mathilde and Justine. Then Justine shooed my stepsisters across the hall to their mother, giving Old Mathilde and me a moment alone. Carefully, Mathilde arranged the lace upon my hair, securing it in place with two jeweled clips studded with stones the same green color as my eyes.

"These belonged to your mother," she said, as she slid them into place. "I have saved them for you until now."

She turned me to face the mirror, and it seemed to me that a stranger gazed back. I did not know this girl in her fine gown. As if she sensed my sudden uncertainty, Old Mathilde came to stand behind me, so that the mirror reflected us both.

"I have worked and waited many years for a day such as this one," she said softly. "To see the light of Constanze's love shine out into the world once more. You are like the plants in your mother's garden, my Cendrillon. A bulb long hidden underground. But the blossom is all the more beautiful for being unexpected."

Old Mathilde leaned forward then, and kissed me on the cheek. "Do not be afraid to grow."

"I am afraid," I whispered. "But I will not let my fear stop me. I will be my mother's child, and yours. I love you, Mathilde."

"As I love you, my little cinder-child. Hurry now; your family is waiting."

And so the child of cinders went to the ball.

"Remember to keep your back straight when you curtsy to the prince," Anastasia instructed, as the carriage inched its way through the crowded streets. "Incline your head and keep your eyes down."

Inside my fine glass slippers, I wiggled my toes. The carriage turned a corner and the palace came into view. I felt a trickle of unease slide down my spine. During our frantic days of preparation, I had worked hard to push all thoughts of my father to the back of my mind. But soon, we would be at the palace. I would see my father for the very first time.

"Look, there is the palace! How beautiful it is," Amelie cried. Every window was ablaze with light so that the palace itself seemed to shine like the evening star. "Have you ever seen anything so beautiful, Maman?"

"Only my three daughters," Chantal de Saint-Andre replied.

"How is it you always know the right thing to say?" I asked, and earned a chuckle.

"I hardly think I do that," my stepmother replied. "If I did, I would have found a way to say, *no thank you, Your Majesty,* when it came to marrying your father. Though, if I had, I would never have had you for a daughter. All in all, I am satisfied with my share of the bargain."

"My father will be angry, won't he?" I asked.

My stepmother reached to give my hand a squeeze. "I imagine he will be," she acknowledged. "I also imagine he will not dare to show it. We are here by the king's command. When we obey him, we show we are his loyal subjects."

"Are you not afraid for yourself, then?" I asked.

"No, I am not," Chantal answered after a moment. "I believe it genuinely angered the king when Etienne sent me from court. My family has served His Majesty long and well. I will call on his protection, if I must."

"We're here!" Anastasia cried suddenly. Raoul brought the carriage to a halt before a broad staircase. At once, Niccolo leaped down from his place at the back to open the carriage door. One by one, we alighted behind my stepmother. Niccolo closed the door, stepped back.

"There will not be four more lovely ladies in all the ballroom," he declared. "Do you not think so, Raoul?"

Raoul looked down from his high perch. "I do think so. And I think you will turn all their heads if you stand there admiring them another moment. Come along, Niccolo."

"Send to the stables when you are ready for us," Niccolo said. He resumed his position, Raoul clucked to the horses, and the carriage started off. With my stepmother in the lead, the four of us started up the steps to the palace.

* * *

The ballroom was a sea of faces, a dazzling blur of color and of light. Great ropes of flowers looped down from the ceiling. Mirrored sconces lined the walls. Courtiers in their best attire jostled for position at the edges of the room. In a whirl of skirts and fancy footwork, couples performed an elaborate dance in a far corner. Snaking through the center was a line of young women, looking like jewels in a necklace in their colorful, shimmering finery. Even as my stomach began to knot in apprehension, I felt a moment of compassion for Prince Pascal.

"I'll bet the prince is wishing his father's kingdom was smaller than it already is," I murmured as we inched our way forward, making our way to the front of the line. My stepmother first, then Anastasia. I came next, with Amelie last in line. I was grateful to be sandwiched between my stepsisters. If not for them, I might have been all too tempted to simply turn tail and run right out the door.

"I hear Gaspard Turenne will be standing beside the prince with a great leather-bound book," Anastasia whispered back. "The name of every eligible maiden will be recorded in it as we all parade by, one by one. If the prince so much as smiles, a special mark is made by that girl's name."

Amelie gave a snort. "Let us hope Monsieur Turenne changed out of his muddy clothes."

We moved a little farther along. I could see a tight knot of courtiers now, those privileged enough to attend the king and

162

queen and prince. Chances were very good my father was one of them. *Don't think about that now,* I told myself. If I thought about my father, I'd never be able to keep on going.

"What happens if Prince Pascal wants to ask someone to dance?" I asked instead, keeping up the game Anastasia had started.

"Then she gets two marks beside her name," Amelie supplied in a low voice. "And a circle around it besides. After all, an invitation to dance is practically a proposal of marriage."

Anastasia gave a gurgle of suppressed laughter.

"Girls," murmured my stepmother. "Behave yourselves."

We took another few steps, and suddenly the space before us opened up. I had a glimpse of glittering garments, jewels gleaming in circlets of gold. And then Chantal was sinking into a deep and graceful curtsy, with Anastasia right behind her. Mindful of my stepsister's endless instructions, I was careful to keep my back straight and my eyes lowered as I, too, sank down.

"But how is this, Etienne?" I heard a woman's voice exclaim. "I thought we were to be denied the pleasure of seeing your wife and daughters tonight."

"I thought so, too, Your Highness," a man's deep voice replied. "I am delighted to be proved wrong." From the corner of my eye, I could see Chantal's skirts move as she began to rise. My heart was pounding so loudly I could hardly believe the whole room didn't echo with the sound.

That is my father's voice, I thought. Polished, with a fine-honed edge, just like a knife.

163

"Madam," Etienne de Brabant went on smoothly. "This is a most welcome surprise."

"I am happy to hear you say so, my lord," my stepmother answered, her own voice calm and even. I tried to hold its cadence in my mind. *She is so strong,* I thought. Precisely what I would need to be, what I wished to be. "We were delighted to receive His Majesty's summons. It is always our pleasure to obey the king in all things," she went on.

"Chantal," I heard a voice that could only be the king's say now. "You are most welcome back to court. No, no—stop bobbing up and down. And here are those lovely daughters of yours. I have been singing their praises to Pascal ever since he arrived."

"All of my daughters are here, Majesty," my stepmother answered. "Including one I think you do not know. Girls."

In front of me, Anastasia began to rise from her curtsy. I followed suit, though my body felt stiff and clumsy. A strange coldness seemed to grip all my limbs, put there by the sound of my father's voice. I hoped my legs would hold me.

"Your Majesties, may I present to you my stepdaughter?" Chantal went on. "She is named Constanze, after her mother, but those of us who love her call her Cendrillon."

"Oh, but she is lovely," I heard the queen's voice exclaim. "The very image of her mother, if I recall. Where have you kept her hidden all this time, Etienne?" She gave a laugh like a chime of silver bells on a winter's day, beautiful yet cold.

"Oh, dear," she went on, her tone playful. "We have made

her nervous with all this attention, I'm afraid. Stop blushing and look up, child."

I can't, I thought. Every single part of my body seemed frozen in its present position.

Then I felt Anastasia slip her arm through mine. At the exact same time, Amelie did the same, and in that moment, the strange cold which had seized me at the first sound of my father's voice abruptly loosed its hold. Warmth flooded through me.

My wish has finally come true, I thought. *I have a mother and sisters to love me, a mother and sisters whom I love.* We were all together, a family united. I lifted my head, and looked into my father's eyes for the very first time.

He was handsome. I could see that at once. Fair-haired and blue-eyed. But in his face, I could see no expression, nothing to inspire the look that gazed so lovingly from out of my mother's portrait. Etienne de Brabant's face was as closed as the door he had locked so long ago. There would be no love for me from him at this late date. As he had begun, so my father would carry on.

Ever so slowly, Etienne de Brabant extended his hand. I placed mine into it, even as I curtsied once more. He pressed his lips to my knuckles for a fraction of a second.

"My daughter," he said. "You are welcome to court."

"Thank you," I said. "My lord." For I discovered that my mouth would not, could not, shape the word *father*. Not for this man.

"Come now," I heard the king say, and, at the sound of his

165

voice, I suddenly found the courage to look into his face. It was open and kind. It was easy to see why my stepmother would give her allegiance to such a man.

"You will have time for reunions later. We must not forget why we are here tonight. Pascal." He made a gesture and a young man dressed in soft gray velvet stepped to his side. On his brow was a circlet of silver set with moonstone. Beside me, I heard Anastasia stifle a sound.

And then my eyes were on the prince's face, a face I knew as well as I did my own. There was the hair, dark as a raven's wing, the storm cloud–colored eyes. They were staring into mine with a startled expression as if, in my own face, he was seeing things he had not known existed before.

"Oh," I said. "Oh, of course."

And only when I saw his expression change did I realize that I had spoken aloud. A great roaring seemed to fill my ears. But it was not until I felt myself jostled from behind that I realized it was coming from the crowd in the ballroom and not from the thousands of unanswered questions streaming through my own mind.

A figure pushed its way forward, fell to its knees before Prince Pascal. Even as it did, the guards surrounding the royal party surged forward, their swords singing in their sheaths as they were drawn. My own body moved as if of its own volition. I dropped to my knees, shielding the body of the figure on the floor with my own.

"No! You must not!" I cried out. "He means no harm."

"Stand away," I heard the prince's voice command.

"Your Highness," protested the captain of the guards. He had been the first to react, the tip of his sword no more than a hand's breadth away from my throat.

"Stand away," the prince said once more, his voice as bright and sharp as the swords drawn in his protection. "Step aside."

"Do as my son says," the king said in a firm, low voice.

Reluctantly, the guards fell back. At a gesture from the captain, several moved to push the crowd back, then stood behind my stepmother and sisters, so that we were all surrounded by a ring of unsheathed swords.

"Let me see your face," the prince said. "Do not be afraid, but look up."

Raoul lifted up his head, and all who saw his features gasped aloud. For a space of time impossible to measure, the two young men stared at each other.

"So," Raoul whispered. "My wish has come true at last."

Then he pitched forward, flat on his face, at the feet of his twin brother.

Fifteen

"I TRIED TO STOP HIM," NICCOLO SAID, HIS VOICE CRACKING with the strain of his distress. "I swear, I tried. The moment I saw the prince's face, I thought I understood why Etienne de Brabant finally ordered Raoul to court."

Several hours later, we were all still at the palace, still in our finery, for, as yet, we had no other clothes. At the king's command, my stepmother's household had been given a special suite of rooms, separate from those of my father. Raoul's sudden appearance had put an end to the evening's festivities.

"To bring about what actually happened," I spoke up, not quite sure I recognized the sound of my own voice.

How could it be safe to feel I recognized anyone anymore?

In the blink of an eye, my childhood companion had become a prince. And I was the daughter of the man who had known this, and concealed it, all along. Who had taken an innocent baby and left him to grow up ignorant of what he was, reducing him to nothing more than a political pawn.

"To disrupt the king's plans for Prince Pascal to marry by revealing the fact that there are two princes, not just one," I went on. I turned to Niccolo, who was standing beside Amelie. She had an arm around his waist, as if to show her support. Their love glowed as brightly as any candle in the room, the one bright and steady spot in an otherwise turbulent night.

"What was it you said the queen has always vowed?" I asked Niccolo.

"That she would never be satisfied until the first son of her heart and blood sits on her husband's throne," he replied.

"A vow which made no sense," I said, "when there was only Prince Pascal. But if there was another son, hidden away since birth, put into the care of the one person in all this land the queen trusts the most. And if that son . . ."

I swallowed against the sudden taste of bile at the back of my throat. "If that son were the first born . . ."

"Oh, but that is wicked!" Anastasia said suddenly, speaking for the first time. "To rob one son of his right, to deny the other all knowledge of who he is for so very long. How can any good come of this? The queen will break Raoul's heart."

"Not to mention the king's," my stepmother chimed in softly. "He loves Pascal very much."

"But how did you and Niccolo come to be in the ballroom in the first place?" Amelie asked. "I thought you were going to wait in the stables."

Niccolo nodded. "We did plan that," he acknowledged. "But Raoul was restless and edgy. He wanted to see what was happening at the ball. He wished to see all of you, I think."

He glanced at me, his expression hesitant, as if uncertain of how I would react to what he was about to reveal. I gave a nod.

"But most of all, he wished to see you, Cendrillon. He was excited for you, worried for you, proud of you, all at once. I tried to talk him out of it. He wouldn't budge. So . . ." Niccolo paused and took a breath.

"I snuck him into the palace, onto one of the balconies overlooking the ballroom. We saw you greet your father, Cendrillon. Then the king made a gesture, a young man who could only be the prince stepped forward, and it was as if both Raoul and I had been turned to stone. He was off and running as if the hounds of hell were at his heels almost before I knew he'd left my side. I could not catch up with him. I'm sorry."

"Don't be," I said quietly. "Even if you had managed to catch him, Raoul would have found some way to keep on going. His whole life, he's wanted to know who he is, wished for this one thing more than anything else. Once he had seen Prince Pascal's face, I don't think anything on earth could have stopped him."

And what of Prince Pascal himself? I wondered. How did he feel about the fact that he had a brother, an identical twin? My stepmother had worried about the king's heart, Anastasia and I worried about Raoul's. Was there no one to worry over Prince Pascal's heart?

My stepmother stood up. "One thing is for certain," she said. "We won't do anyone any good by staying up and worrying all night. A good night's sleep is in order, I think. Perhaps things will look less dire in the morning."

"What about Old Mathilde?" I asked. "Shouldn't we try and get word to her?"

"I have been thinking about that." Chantal nodded. "I think it is best to say nothing about the fact that she is in the city, for now. When we know more about what may happen, then we can decide what to do. But she should be told what has occurred tonight. It concerns her."

"I will take a message to her," Niccolo offered.

"I was hoping you would say that," my stepmother acknowledged. "But be careful of how you come and go, Niccolo. When you are with us, you are under the king's protection. But when you are on your own . . ."

"I will take care," he promised, and I saw the way that Amelie's arms tightened. She saw him to the door. When she turned back to face the room, her face was wet with tears.

"Maman," she began.

Her mother moved to her quickly, silencing her with an

arm around her shoulders. "I know, *ma petite*," she said. "I know. I see what you feel for him, and he for you. Niccolo is clever and resourceful. He will stay out of danger. Take heart. All will yet be well."

"Then you do not disapprove?" Amelie asked.

"Of course not," her mother answered with a smile. "I like him very well. And he will be just the one to take you on all those adventures you've always dreamed about." She turned back to Anastasia and me. "Come," she said. "Let us all go to bed."

Anastasia moved at once to her mother's side.

"I will stay up for a few moments longer, if I may," I said. I didn't think I'd be able to sleep if my life depended on it.

"Of course," said my stepmother. "Try not to worry too much about Raoul. If nothing else, he is now too valuable to come to any harm." Together, the three of them vanished into the sleeping chambers.

I sat in a chair by the window, watching the play of candle-light upon the stone of the palace walls, so different from the stone of the walls at home. *So much has happened,* I thought. *And yet so little time has gone by.*

A thousand images seemed to crowd for space inside my head. Raoul as a boy, fuming over some imagined insult, laughing at some unexpected joy. Standing beside me at my mother's grave each and every year on the birthday that we shared, making the same wish, asking the same question, over and over: *Who am I?*

And now, that question had been answered and nothing would ever be the same. Not for Raoul. Not for any of us.

All of a sudden, large as it was, the room seemed too small, the air within it stifling. The palace itself seemed to bear down upon me. No longer beautiful, but a trap that had snatched my oldest friend away and would send him back a stranger.

I want to get out of here, I thought. Without stopping to think, I leaped to my feet and ran to the door. Pulling it open, I dashed into the corridor. And then I was simply running, flying along the hallways of the palace on glass-slippered feet, not knowing, not caring where I was going. The journey, not the destination, was all that mattered. The sense of freedom, never mind that it was false, that always comes with motion.

Eventually, my headlong race carried me to the top of a wide and curving set of stairs and here, at last, my feet slowed and stopped. Below me stretched the ballroom I had been so nervous to enter, just a few short hours ago. The air was thick here, too, this time with the scent of flowers. The garlands of them were still in place, but they were drooping now. The candles guttered in their sconces. Only a few still flickered along the walls. I set my hands upon the balustrade, felt the cool of the stone through my palms.

"Cendrillon," I thought I heard a voice say, floating like a phantom on the air, and at the sound of it, I started.

"Who is it? Who is there?" I called.

In answer to my question, a figure below me stepped into a

patch of light. I had not noticed him before, for he was dressed in clothing almost the same shade as the shadows which surrounded him. He tilted his face up. At the sight of it, I caught my breath.

It was Prince Pascal.

Sixteen

"YOUR HIGHNESS," I SAID, AS I BEGAN TO SINK INTO A CURTSY.

"Oh, don't," he said, bringing my motion to a halt. "Please. It's just us. I wonder—I would like to speak with you, if I might. Will you come down?"

I opened my mouth to say I couldn't, then changed my mind. There was something in the sound, the timbre of his voice, that I had heard before. Raoul had always sounded just like this when he was asking for something he wished for very much, so much he was almost afraid to ask in case the answer would be no.

"Of course I will come down, if that is what you wish," I said.

"It is," the prince replied. Slowly, carefully, I descended the stairs, my skirts whispering around me as if telling secrets. I reached the bottom and the prince materialized at my side. He extended an arm, bent at the elbow. I placed my own upon it and stepped off the stair, onto the ballroom floor.

"Thank you," he said simply. Then, as if suddenly realizing he wasn't sure quite what to do now that he had convinced me to join him, he began to lead me around the ballroom, for all the world, as if we were taking an afternoon stroll in the park.

"You knew me," Prince Pascal said after a moment. "You did not mistake me for . . ." His voice faltered for a fraction of a second before it went on. "My brother."

"Of course not," I said at once. "Surely no one who truly knew either of you could mistake one for the other."

"And you believe you know him truly?" the prince inquired.

"I believe I know him as well as anyone else does," I answered. We reached a junction of the ballroom walls. Pascal put a hand to my waist, and gently guided me out into the middle of the room. "I've known him since he was two weeks old."

"The age he was when your father brought him to your estate," the prince filled in, and now I heard the temper of steel in his voice. Young though he was, he would not be a good man to cross, I thought. And I remembered suddenly what Niccolo had said: that Pascal was loved wherever he traveled, that the people found him fair and just.

I nodded. "That is so."

"What of the future?" the prince asked.

I frowned. "I'm sorry," I said. "I don't understand what you are asking."

"You and Raoul," Pascal said. "What do you hope for now? You must be childhood sweethearts, with a story like that."

I gave a quick peal of laughter before I could stop myself. "Whatever gave you that idea?" I inquired. "Raoul is in love with my stepsister Anastasia, to tell you the truth. A somewhat complicated and unhappy state of affairs until tonight's . . ." I paused, searching for the right word. "Surprise."

"I'm sorry if I've offended you," Prince Pascal said at once. "When you moved so quickly to protect him, I naturally thought . . ."

"I am not in the least offended," I answered. "I am also not the least bit in love with Raoul."

"I see," Pascal said. We walked in silence for a moment. "I saw you and your stepsisters whispering together as you approached the front of the line," he said. "You were the only girls all evening who showed any sort of real expression at all. Everyone else just looked incredibly hopeful or completely terrified."

"It made me wonder about you before I even knew who you were. It certainly made me wonder what you were talking about."

"Oh," I said, coming to a dead stop as I suddenly remembered what our topic of conversation had been. "Oh, dear. Oh, no. Please don't ask me to tell you."

The prince laughed, the sound surprised, as if laughing was a thing he didn't do very often. "It can't be all that bad. I can command you to tell me, you know."

"That's what I call unfair," I said, at which he laughed once more.

"That's twice you've made me laugh," he said. "I'm afraid I'm going to have to insist."

I shook my head. "Oh, very well. Since you must know, I remarked that the line of eligible maidens seemed so long, I wondered if you were wishing your father ruled a smaller kingdom."

Prince Pascal's lips twitched. "Indeed, I did wish that," he said. "What else?"

"Then Anastasia claimed there was a special book in which the names of all the eligible maidens were being written down. A special mark would be placed by a girl's name if you so much as smiled. And Amelie claimed that, if you asked one to dance, it would be almost as good as a marriage proposal. That's when my stepmother told us to hush."

Prince Pascal stopped walking. "I wonder," he said, in a tone I could not quite interpret, "if you would care to dance with me now."

"Your Highness," I faltered, then wondered how I had managed to speak at all when my heart had leaped straight into my throat.

"I could insist again," he said. "But I think that I will not.

Instead, I will say please. Will you please do me the honor of dancing with me, Cendrillon? Will you do me the honor of saying my name? For I find that I would like you to do both, very much."

He stepped back and sketched a quick bow, his face tilted downward so that his expression was in shadow. Then he straightened up and held out a hand. I placed trembling fingers within it.

"It would be my pleasure to dance with you, Pascal," I said. And I stepped forward, into his arms.

Here, oh, here, I thought, as we began to move in small, then great, sweeping circles, my skirts flying out, the brilliants catching the moonlight as Pascal and I danced across the ballroom floor.

This was the feeling, the certainty, that I had not found in Raoul's arms—the deep and absolute belief that here, at last, was where I belonged. I was filled with the sudden knowledge that I had been searching my whole life for just this moment, just this feeling, and all without realizing I had been searching at all.

I saw Pascal's face change then, saw something kindle deep within his storm-tossed eyes. A thing so bright and pure it let me see my own gaze reflected in it, and instantly, I knew the truth: I was gazing into the face of joy. This was what my mother had seen within my father's face, the look that I had been able only to imagine until now. The sheer surprise, unbridled wonder, and exquisite joy of unexpected love. Love at first sight.

"Cendrillon," Pascal said. "I . . ."

My footsteps faltered then, as one of my glass slippers encountered something smooth and slick, spent flower petals that had fallen to the ballroom floor. I felt my ankle twist, my foot slip from the shoe, just as Pascal lifted me up, leaving the shoe behind. And then I stopped caring about shoes and feet, stopped thinking of anything at all. For Pascal's arms around me were both gentle and tight, and then his lips found mine.

Sweet, so very sweet, I thought. Sweet and firm and strong. I kissed him back, kissed him as I had dreamed of being kissed, but had never quite believed I might be. *It is all decided now,* I thought. I had wondered who would be the one to worry over what was in Prince Pascal's heart, and now I knew the truth: It was me.

Slowly, slowly, Pascal set me on my feet. But before either of us could say a word, there came another voice, one I thought I recognized.

"My apologies for interrupting you, Your Highness," said my father's voice, and once again, I was reminded of the blade of a knife. "But your lady mother is asking for you."

All trace of what he was feeling vanished from Pascal's face. It went completely blank, as if he had drawn a curtain across whatever might be inside. I felt a sudden pang of loneliness seize my heart. *I have only just found you,* I thought. *Don't go yet. Don't go.*

"Thank you for your care, my lord de Brabant," the prince said. "Please be so good as to inform my mother I will be with her in a moment."

"With your permission, I would be happy to escort my daughter back to her rooms," offered my father. "She is a stranger to the palace and might lose her way otherwise."

At this, finally, Pascal stepped back. "As always, your suggestions are most reasonable, my lord. Thank you for your care." He bowed over my hand, the faintest brush of his lips across the backs of my knuckles. "I will look forward to seeing you tomorrow, Cendrillon."

He turned and left without another word. My father stepped forward. For several humming moments, the two of us regarded each other.

"It would seem that you are to be congratulated," Etienne de Brabant said at last. "I doubt that the prince will so much as look at anyone else now."

"I don't know what you mean," I said.

My father made a curt, dismissive gesture. "Do not play the fool with me," he said, his voice not quite so smooth and polished now. "Surely you cannot be so naïve, even if you are country-bred. You have made a conquest, and you should be proud of it. But neither of you is sitting on a throne quite yet. If I were you, I wouldn't count on it."

He moved then, before I realized what he intended, giving me no time to step back. He caught me by the shoulders, leaning close to study my face, then released me and stepped back.

"You are not quite what I expected you might be," he pronounced at last. "And Pascal's attraction to you is certainly unexpected. Perhaps we may be of some use to each other yet before all this is done."

I stood perfectly still, staring at him. "Why should I wish to be of any use to you?" I inquired in a tone like ice. "I have seen my mother's face, seen the portrait in her room, and so I know how much she loved you. If she could look upon you now, I wonder if she would recognize the man you have become. If someone painted her face tonight, what expression would it show, I wonder?"

I brushed past him, moving up the stairs, doing my best to keep my back straight and my head held high. An affect that was almost spoiled by the fact that I was wearing only one shoe, a fact my father's presence had nearly driven from my mind. *I will not go back for it,* I thought. *I will not go back at all.*

"You may not speak so to me," Etienne de Brabant said as I reached the top of the stairs, and now his voice was fierce and hard, as if everything he had felt for the last sixteen years, all the things he had denied, were clenched tight as a fist inside him, and now the fist was pounding, demanding to be let out. "I am your father."

"And I am your daughter," I replied, as I turned back after all. "The one you never wanted. You have blamed me for an act not of my making, not of my desire, every single day of my life. Aside from courtesy, my lord, what is it that you think I owe you? I will not be made a pawn in your games. I will find my own way back. Good night."

I turned, and left him standing in the ballroom.

Seventeen

WHEN I GOT BACK TO MY ROOM, RAOUL WAS THERE, HOVERING like a ghost outside the door.

"Cendrillon," he said when he saw me, and I heard the way his voice broke, whether in joy or sorrow I could not tell.

"Raoul," I said, as I caught him to me. For a moment, we clung together. "How are you?" I asked at last. "Are you well?"

"Well enough," he said. He gave a shaky laugh as he let me go. "In fact, I—"

He broke off with a glance over his shoulder, and only then did I realize that a guard such as the ones I had seen in the ballroom stood several paces down the hall.

"Come inside," I said. "You can do that, can't you?"

"I'm a prince now," Raoul said, though I could tell by his voice that he did not quite believe it, even now. "Within reason, I can do whatever I want."

"Then come in," I said. "Let's stop skulking in the hall."

I opened the door to our rooms, ushered him inside, then closed the door behind us. The large common room was empty, my stepmother and stepsisters having gone to bed. Candles still burned on several low tables, and in the window enclosure. Raoul moved restlessly around the room, finally coming to a halt before the window, gazing out at the city below.

"The lights are still burning in the windows of the town," he said. "How can so many things have happened and yet it isn't even midnight?"

"What has happened?" I asked, as I sat down upon a padded stool. "Tell me."

"I've been speaking with all of them," he said. "My father." His voice stumbled slightly on the word. "My mother and brother. Do you have any idea what it's like to look into someone else's face and see your own gazing back?"

"No," I answered quietly. "Everyone says I look like my mother, but it's not the same thing."

"I have been given my own suite of rooms," Raoul said. "Not far from Prince Pascal's. A guard to keep me safe."

"Safe," I said. "From what?"

Raoul turned to face me then, and I could see the strange and tortured expression in his eyes.

"I have just come from speaking with the queen," he said. "She wanted us to speak, privately. No one was present, except for your father. She says, the queen, my mother says . . ." Raoul's voice faltered, then steadied. "That I am the elder son. That is why your father took me, all those years ago. To keep me safe. It is I who should be king when my father dies and not Pascal."

So, I thought. *It is as my stepmother and Niccolo thought.* The queen would try to place Raoul upon the throne. Use him to perform a coup, now that her brother's armies had been destroyed.

What kind of a woman could do such a thing? I wondered. To achieve her own ambition, she had deprived one son of his childhood birthright. Now she would pit him against the brother he had barely begun to know. If she broke the king's heart in the process, so much the better. And Etienne de Brabant had been her instrument. My father, who no longer seemed to have any heart at all.

She does not care about you, Raoul, I thought. *All she cares about is that we are all under her control.*

"You say you have just come from her?" I said. "She has just sent for Pascal. I wonder how she will tell him what she has told you."

"You have seen the prince?" Raoul asked, surprised. And I could not help but notice that, in spite of what he now believed he could claim for himself, he still spoke as if there was only one.

I nodded. "I came from him just now. We did not plan to meet. It just sort of . . . happened."

Before I understood what he intended, Raoul crossed the room and caught my face between his hands, tilting it toward the candlelight.

"You love him!" he exclaimed. "I can see it in your face. You met him for the first time tonight, and yet you love him already."

"It didn't take you much longer to fall in love with Anastasia," I remarked. "Let go, Raoul. You're pinching my chin. Besides, you know what I look like."

"No," he said, drawing out the syllable as he released me. "I don't think I do. Not altogether. Not quite." He stepped back, but his eyes stayed on my face. "Does it hurt, this newfound love?"

"I haven't decided yet," I admitted.

"Does he love you?"

"I think he does."

"You might be queen someday, then," Raoul said. "If not for me."

"Oh, will you stop being so stupid?" I exclaimed crossly, as I stood up. "I don't care about that and you should know it. Neither will you, if you are smart. You have only the queen's word about the fact that you are firstborn, Raoul. If she's demonstrated anything, it's that she's someone it's not safe to trust.

"What will you do if Pascal and your father object to this

sudden rearranging of things? Will you fight them?"

"I don't know what I'll do!" Raoul cried out, his voice anguished. "How can I? For as long as I can remember, I've wished for just one thing, and you know it as well as I do. The same thing, year in, year out. Now, in the blink of an eye, my wish has been answered. I know who I am. I woke up a stable boy, but I'll go to bed a prince. Who is to say that I might not be king one day besides?"

"So you would fight," I said. "You would make war on your father and brother. The queen will have no more need for foreign mercenaries. She will get you to do her fighting for her."

"Rilla," Raoul said, and at the sound of my childhood nickname, my heart gave a pang. "Don't I have the right to claim what is mine?"

"Of course you do," I said. I went to him, my feet awkward with only one shoe, and laid a hand upon his arm. I felt the way his own trembled as he laid it over mine. "But surely not at any cost. That day we stood in the pumpkin patch and saw the ships, we made a wish together, the only time we've ever wished for the same thing in all our lives. We wished to find a way to make the fighting stop.

"The queen is just trying to use you, don't you see? She doesn't love you any more than my father loves me. She is the one who has deprived you of your birthright, not your father or brother. She sent you away, when she should have kept you close."

Raoul stood absolutely motionless, staring down at me with devastated eyes. "I thought you would be happy for me," he said. "I thought you would want what I want."

"Not if it means you're going to fight your own brother, Raoul," I said. "Not if it means starting a war and tearing the country apart."

"It's because you love him, isn't it?" he asked. He dropped his hand from my arm and stepped away. "It's because you love Pascal."

"It's because I love *you*," I said at once. "Of course I am happy that you have finally discovered who you really are. But I can hardly rejoice if you plan to fight the father and brother you've only just found. How can that be what you want for yourself? How can that be who you truly are?"

"I don't have to explain myself to you," Raoul said.

"No," I replied. "You don't. But no matter who you are, you are answerable to yourself."

"You'll go to him, won't you?" he suddenly challenged. "As soon as I leave this room, you'll go to Pascal. You'll find him and warn him."

"I honestly don't know what I'll do." I sighed. "You're my oldest and dearest friend, Raoul. I have loved you for almost as long as I have been alive. Don't ask me to choose between an old love and the new. That's no choice at all, and in your heart, you know it."

I watched the struggle come and go across his face. "I

will think about what you have said," Raoul answered finally. "Please—I would like to ask you to do nothing tonight. Please wait, give me time to think, and let us speak again in the morning."

"Is it the new prince or my old friend who asks me this?" I said.

"It is both," Raoul replied. "I'm trying to find the way to make them both fit inside my skin. It's harder than I thought. I haven't learned how to be both yet. Please, Rilla. Give me some time."

"Very well," I said. "I will give you until tomorrow, as you ask."

"Thank you, Rilla," Raoul said. "You are a good friend."

"And you are good at getting your own way," I replied.

For a moment, I thought he would say something more, then I saw the way his eyes shifted to take in something over my shoulder.

"It must be midnight," he said. "The lights are going out."

I turned to face the city then, and saw that he was right. Through the window of our suite of rooms, I could see the lights in the town below us begin to go out, one by one. Then, as if a great wind had suddenly come up, the streets went dark, all at once. I felt a quick shiver slide straight down my back.

It looks like an omen, I thought. Of what, I wasn't sure I cared to guess.

I turned back toward Raoul, and heard the click of the closing door.

"He's gone, isn't he?" Anastasia's voice said.

"Yes," I said. "He's gone." I turned to face her, saw the tears upon her cheeks. "If you love him, go after him," I said. "Don't let him go."

"How can I?" she said in a low and tortured voice. "I made so much of the differences between us. What will he think if I go after him now?"

"You'll never know unless you do it," I said. "Help him, Anastasia. Don't throw away love."

"I'll never understand why you don't hate me," she said. "But I'll tell you this. I'm grateful that you don't."

She moved swiftly to the door and pulled it open. "Raoul," she called in a low voice.

The moment she stepped into the hall, I knew he had turned back. Anastasia darted forward, and I moved to stand in the open door. I saw the way she moved toward him swiftly, then faltered. And as she did, Raoul stepped forward in his turn, and pulled her into his arms. She put her head upon his shoulder. He, an arm around her waist. Entirely heedless of the guard who still stood several respectful paces off, they moved off together down the hall.

I'll never know what made me sense the danger. A change in the air, perhaps. A strange scent. An unexpected hint of sound. It didn't matter, as it turned out. Because I wasn't quick enough. Before I quite realized what was happening, something thick and dark and stifling was being thrown over my head. Strong arms banded around mine from behind. I felt myself being lifted, kicked out once, and felt my second shoe go flying. I heard the chime of broken glass as it crashed to the floor.

And then, nothing.

Eighteen

IT WAS ANASTASIA WHO FIRST TOLD ME THE STORY OF WHAT happened next, who helped me see what I could not. How, after settling things between them, pledging to love each other now and forever, no matter who they were or might become, she and Raoul had walked back to the rooms we shared and there discovered the heel of one glass shoe and a scatter of broken glass outside our door.

When a quick and frantic search failed to produce any additional sign of me, Raoul did not hesitate, but, accompanied by my stepmother and stepsisters, went directly to the king and Prince Pascal. He told them of the queen's treachery, of his fear that my father had seized me and carried me from the palace. The king sent for my father at once. When he did not answer the summons, when he, too, could not be found, Raoul knew his worst fears had been realized.

"Where would he take her?" Pascal asked, the fear in his eyes and in his voice telling anyone with eyes and ears of their own all they needed to know about what was in his heart. "He could be anywhere by now. Where would he go?"

"I think I know the answer to that," Raoul had said. "He will take her to the great stone house by the sea. He will take her home."

"Then we must go after her at once," Pascal said.

"If I may, Your Highness." Amelie had surprised them all by speaking up. At a gesture from Pascal to continue, she turned to Raoul. "You should take Niccolo. He will want to help. And he knows the road better than you do."

"That is a good thought," Raoul said at once. "And let us send for Old Mathilde." He turned back to Pascal. "She raised Cendrillon. No one knows her better or loves her more."

"I will trust your judgment in this," Pascal said.

And so Niccolo and Mathilde were sent for. As soon as they arrived, the party set off, the two princes and Niccolo taking swift horses and riding ahead, my stepmother, my stepsisters, and Old Mathilde following in a carriage. Only the king stayed behind. His first act once the others had departed was to see that the queen was close confined. Save for the members of her immediate household, all carefully selected by the king, she was never seen in public again.

The story I told in return goes like this: that I awakened to find myself slung across the back of my father's horse like an unwanted parcel. All that night, and all the day that followed, Etienne de Brabant spurred his horse along the road. His only concession to my presence was to allow me to sit up behind him once he knew I was awake.

Just before nightfall at the end of the second day, we came to the great stone house. The journey had taken a full day less than the one that had brought me to the palace in the first place, so great was my father's desire to reach his destination. Etienne de Brabant dismounted, pulled me from the horse, carried me up the steps. With one booted foot, he kicked open the front door, all but scaring the wits out of Susanne, who had come to see what all the commotion was about, and had gotten no farther than the great hall.

At a sharp command, she scurried to get out of the way. My father set me down. Then, with a yank that had my head rocking on my shoulders, he set off across the great hall and up the stairs that led to the second story. Down the corridor to the very end we went, until at last we stood outside my mother's door.

"Open it," he commanded.

But I heard what was in his voice. I had been frightened when my father first seized me, and for many moments on our long, wild ride. But I was not afraid of anything within the great stone house, not even him, and it was fear that I heard inside my father's voice. Fear of what he had tried, without success, to lock away from the world, and from himself. And so I lifted my chin and stepped back.

"I am not the one who is afraid of what lies beyond that door," I said. "Open it yourself."

He started then, staring at me as if seeing me for the very first time. Not as what he had imagined for nearly sixteen long years, but as what I truly was: Constanze d'Este's daughter, his own true child. For the time it took my heart to beat six times, he did not move. Then, slowly, my father reached out, seized the latch, lifted it up, and opened my mother's bedroom door.

Gone were the cobwebs, the dust that had greeted me on my first glimpse of this room. Old Mathilde and I had taken down the bedhangings and the curtains to launder and iron them. We had scrubbed the floors and washed the windows till they shone. In the glow of twilight, the room looked warm and welcoming, as if its occupant had stepped out of it just minutes before. Slowly, his feet making absolutely no sound, my father crossed the room until he reached the alcove. I knew the second he saw my mother's face. He faltered back a step, then stood as still as stone.

"She loved you," I said from where I stood within the open door. "You can see it in her eyes. Old Mathilde told me once that a love that strong and pure never really dies. It lives on in all who live and remember, teaching them how to discover such a love for themselves. I try to imagine how I would feel if I had known a love like that, then had it snatched away. All my life, I've tried to understand how you could love her, and not love me.

"But when I look into her face, I cannot do it. I do not understand it at all. Constanze d'Este loved you, and all you might create together. You thought you loved her, but you loved yourself more."

I pointed to the window behind him, and, as if my gesture was a summons, my father slowly turned around.

"From that window, you can see my mother's grave, the only piece of earth on all your lands where not a single living thing will thrive. But it is not my mother's heart that is buried there. Instead, I think that it is yours."

With a cry my father whirled back, strode across the room to seize me by the arms. He pulled me to the window, turning me so that I, too, looked down.

"I have carried the image of your mother's grave with me for sixteen years," he said fiercely. "Nothing I have ever done has been able to drive it from my mind. Don't think you can stand there and lecture me. You can never understand what I have lost."

"You did not lose!" I cried, as I struck his hands away. For the first time, I thought I tasted his bitterness in my own mouth. "You gave it away of your own free will. You gave *me* away. You gave away love."

And because of it, he had wasted the span of my entire life, I thought. What might my father and I have learned together, shared together, if he had not been so swift to give up on love? Regret shot through me then, swift and sudden as the plunge of a knife straight through my heart. I staggered, and put my hand upon the windowsill. Felt my father reach to hold me up.

Oh, Mathilde, I thought. *I see what you were trying to tell me now, that day in the kitchen so long ago.*

Grief and sorrow are one and the same. But until you feel regret for what is now forever out of reach, you do not truly mourn.

Finally, I felt my anger for my father turn to ashes. I saw the desolation in his face now. Saw the way it ran bone-deep.

"I know what you wished for me," I said softly. "The one and only time you ever saw me until now. You wished that you might never see me again unless the sight of me could give you back the peace I stole. But I am not the true thief, father. You have robbed yourself. You have no peace because you cling to sorrow and to anger.

"You have no peace because you do not mourn."

"No," Etienne de Brabant answered, with a shuddering breath. "No. That cannot be right; it cannot be so."

"Go to my mother's grave," I said. "Kneel down beside it. Feel the dead grass with your hand. Place your palm on the dead trunk of the tree Constanze d'Este planted as your bride. Then tell me you have no regrets. That you do not see all the things that you have stolen from us both, but from yourself most of all.

"Then do what, in my heart, I think my mother would have wished. Make a new wish for yourself."

He released me then, his movement so unexpected that, had I not caught the back of the chair, I might have tumbled to the floor. Without a backward glance my father ran from the bedroom, down the corridor. I heard the clatter of his boots as he hastened down the great hall stairs, the sound of the front door as it opened, then slammed closed.

Slowly, I sank down in the chair, the one in which Old Mathilde had sat the night I had been born. Gazing out the window, by the light of the moon, I saw my father stagger to my mother's graveside. He fell down upon his knees, lifted his face up to the heavens as he had so many years ago. Perhaps it was some trick of the light, but I swear that, even from the second-story window, I saw the tracks of tears upon his cheeks. After sixteen years, my father wept beside my mother's grave, while I wept to see him, looking down.

I will make a wish for you, Father, I thought. The fourth most powerful kind of wish there is. One you make when you discover that, against all odds and appearances to the contrary, you have not quite given up hope after all.

I wish that the tears you shed may make what you wished for sixteen years ago come true. I wish you peace, at last.

Nineteen

LATE THAT NIGHT, I HEARD THE SOUND OF HORSES IN THE courtyard. Long before then, I had moved through every room on the ground floor in the great stone house, placing a lighted candle in every single window, as if to guide travelers home. Outside, the moon was gold and full, its light bright enough to read a book by.

I changed out of my bedraggled ballroom finery into one of the dresses my stepmother and I had made over for me. With my hair braided and pinned on top of my head, a pair of sturdy and practical shoes on my feet, I felt like myself once more.

"Cendrillon!" I heard Raoul's voice cry out above the sound of the horse's hooves. "Cendrillon!"

I flung open the front door, flew down the steps. He leaped from his horse to swing me around in a great circle, my legs flying.

"I knew you would know what to do," I said. "I knew you would come."

Raoul set me on my feet. "You lighted candles just like they do in the city," he said. "It's beautiful. I didn't come alone."

It was only at that moment that I realized there were two other horses in the courtyard. Niccolo sat upon one. This, I might have expected. What I did not expect was that the third rider should be Prince Pascal. I felt my heart perform a long, slow somersault inside my chest.

"You came together," I said. "Oh, Raoul." I threw my arms around him.

"I may be an idiot on occasion," Raoul whispered in my ear. "But at least I can admit when I've been wrong. Besides, you are more important than any crown. Now stop hugging me. Your prince will get the wrong idea about us."

He stepped back. "Is Susanne still up?" he asked aloud.

"She is in the kitchen waiting for you," I said. "If I know her, she started frying rashers of bacon the second she heard horses' hooves in the courtyard. She took a cherry pie out of the oven not half an hour ago."

Raoul gave a shout of laughter and sprinted for the kitchen door. Niccolo tossed a leg over the saddle and slid lightly to the ground. He came to me and caught me by the hands.

"You don't look any worse for wear," he said. "It gives me joy to see that you are well."

"Thank you, Niccolo," I said. "And I hope I will be calling you brother before too long."

He leaned forward and kissed me on the cheek. "I hope so too," he replied. "Your mother and sisters send their love. They should be here sometime tomorrow. Old Mathilde is with them."

He moved past me into the house. Now it was just Pascal and me in the courtyard. In the moonlight, I could see every plane and angle of his face, but I could not read what his expression held.

"You have just had a long, hard ride," I said at last. "Don't you at least want to get down?"

Without a word, Pascal swung down from the saddle and came toward me.

"Raoul said you would be here," he said. "That your father would bring you home."

"I don't imagine that he thought of it that way," I answered. "But Raoul was right. My mother is buried in this place. She died the night that I was born. All my life, my father has blamed me for this. He had to bring me here, I think, before he could truly decide what to do with me, or what not to do."

"Where is he?" asked Pascal.

"He is gone. He sat beside my mother's grave until the moon came up, then got on his horse and rode out the gate. I do not think any of us will ever see him again."

"So you are quite safe," Pascal said. "You've been safe for hours. You didn't really need rescuing at all."

"Maybe not," I said. "But I'm glad that you have come."

"Are you?" he asked. "Why?"

"Will you walk with me?" I said, by way of an answer. "There is something I would like to show you."

Giving me an answer of his own, Pascal offered me his arm. I took it and together we walked around the side of the house, along its length, until we reached the gate in the stone wall that was just higher than a tall man's head and led to my mother's garden. I opened the latch, pushed the gate open wide. Then I led Pascal across the soft green lawn until we reached my mother's grave.

It was covered with pumpkin vines. Pansies with brave faces. Bee balm. Every single thing that I had ever tried to grow upon my mother's grave had come to life, watered by my father's tears. Only the tree my mother had planted herself remained unchanged.

"This is the place my mother is buried," I said. "Every year, on my birthday, I have made a wish here for as long as I can recall. And what I wished for was this: that what I planted here might grow and thrive. Tomorrow is my birthday. My wish has finally come true."

"It's beautiful," Pascal said.

"It wasn't," I answered. "Not until tonight. Tonight my

father mourned my mother truly for the very first time. Old Mathilde, who raised me, said my parents loved each other from the moment they met, love at first sight. She says such a talent runs in families, and I think that she is right. For I believe that my heart knew you from the moment you first held me in your arms.

"I wish to be my mother's daughter," I said. "I will make many mistakes, have many regrets, take many risks, but I will not do what my father did. I will not turn my back on love."

"Are you saying that you love me?" Pascal said, and I felt the way his arm trembled beneath my fingers.

"Yes," I replied. "I know it's traditional for the man to speak first, especially when he's a prince, and I know that it is sudden."

"I think," Pascal said carefully, "that I would like to ask you something."

"Anything," I said.

"Will you please sit down?"

"Sit down?" I echoed, altogether stunned.

"Yes," Prince Pascal said. "Here, on this pumpkin."

"Of course I will," I said, but my heart had begun to beat with a sound like thunder. I had just told the handsome prince I'd known for less than three days that I loved him, and he had asked me to sit down upon a pumpkin. At least I knew it would be sturdy enough to hold me.

Remember what you promised yourself, Cendrillon, I thought fiercely. *Never regret love.*

"I went back," Pascal said, as he settled me upon the pumpkin. "To the ballroom. After Etienne had called me away, I got halfway to my mother's rooms and thought . . ."

All of a sudden, he began to pace, just outside the reach of the pumpkin vines. I felt my heartbeats begin to steady. He was not quite as composed as I had thought.

"I thought to myself, *You are an idiot, Pascal!*" he went on. "*You've just held the girl you love, the one you know you want to marry in your arms. And what did you do? You let some smooth-talking courtier take you away, never mind the fact that he's her father.* So I turned around and went back, but by then you were gone."

He stopped pacing and reached inside his coat. From an inside pocket, he removed an object wrapped in cloth. Carefully, as if what he held was infinitely precious, he pulled the cloth aside and let it flutter to the ground.

"I found this in the ballroom. You had gone, but you left this behind. And so I wonder . . ." With a graceful movement, he knelt at my feet. "I wonder if I might persuade you to try on this shoe, so that I can be certain that it fits you, and you alone. Please show me I haven't dreamed this whole thing from start to finish."

Slowly, Prince Pascal reached out. I put my right foot into his hand. He untied the laces of my sturdy, sensible shoe, then eased it off and set it gently on the ground. In its place, he slid on the slipper made of glass.

"Be with me," he said. "Please, Cendrillon. Love me. Let me love you."

"Yes," I said. "Yes to all of it."

He leaned forward then, and kissed me for the second time. And as he did, I felt a band around my heart, one I had grown so accustomed to holding in place that I no longer noticed its presence, open up, loosen its hold. And as it did, my heart flew free.

Behind us, at the head of my mother's grave, the dead tree gave a moan. Catching me to him, Pascal sprang up. With a great crack, the blackened bark split open. A great trembling seized the tree's every limb, and then the bark peeled back like the skin of an onion. Revealing strong new bark beneath, glimmering pale and fresh in the moonlight.

The whole tree seemed to give itself a shake, its limbs reaching upward as if stretching after a dream of standing motionless for far too long. And then, in a rush so full and joyous it almost made a sound, every single branch burst into bloom. Our eyes were filled with the sight of blossoms of pure silver, our noses with a scent as sweet as honey.

"This is why they say love stories end 'happily ever after,'" I whispered. For surely, if this was anything, it was the power of true love. The power to bring life and hope where none had been before.

Hand in hand, Pascal and I left my mother's garden and walked back to the front of the house. As we approached, the candles I had placed in all the downstairs windows flickered, and then went out.

And that is how I knew the truth. My story had been given the start of its happy ending at the very same time in which it had first begun: just before midnight.

The tree above my mother's grave grew and bloomed as the love Pascal and I shared together did, every single day for the rest of our lives. It is blooming there still, for all I know. For Old Mathilde had the right of things. True love never dies.

Author's Note

A FUNNY THING HAPPENED ON THE WAY TO THE BALL.

When my editor and I first discussed the possibility of having me add the story of Cinderella to the Once upon a Time series, I decided it would be interesting to refresh my memory about the early versions of this incredibly famous tale. So I marched to the bookshelf in search of my copy of *The Complete Tales of the Brothers Grimm*. Sure enough, "Cinderella" was there. I thought I knew, in a general sort of way, what to expect. Boy, did I get a surprise. Because almost the first thing their rendition does is mention the fact that Cinderella's father is still alive.

Intrigued, I turned to an even earlier version, that of the French author Charles Perrault (1628–1703), generally considered the father of the modern fairy tale. Like the Grimm boys who came after him (late seventeen hundreds to mid–eighteen hundreds), Perrault draws heavily on older, oral folktale traditions for his stories. Would Cinderella's father show up here as well? The answer was yes.

Okay, I thought. *Wait just a minute here.*

Both renditions do make similar points, that the father falls so under the control of his second wife that he will do whatever she wants. He then pretty much vanishes from the tale completely, leaving Cinderella's stepmother in control. But the fact that he was there at all simply proved too intriguing a notion for me to pass up.

If Cinderella's father is still alive, but takes no action to save or protect her, what might this say about both him and the woman to whom we are all accustomed to assigning the role of the bad guy? What would happen if I put a father back into the mix? With that, my own version of the story was off and running. I decided to add my own tribute to Perrault by giving my heroine the French version of her name: Cendrillon.

About the Author

CAMERON DOKEY is the author of more than thirty young adult novels. Her most recent titles include *The World Above* and *Winter's Child*. She is also the author of *How NOT to Spend Your Senior Year*. Cameron lives in Seattle, Washington.

RIVETED

BY *simon* teen ♥

BELIEVE IN YOUR SHELF

Visit RivetedLit.com & connect with us on social to:

DISCOVER NEW YA READS

READ BOOKS FOR FREE

DISCUSS YOUR FAVORITES

SHARE YOUR IDEAS

ENTER SWEEPSTAKES FOR THE CHANCE TO WIN BOOKS

Follow @SimonTeen on

to stay up to date with all things Riveted!